BEYOND BLACKWATER POND

BEYOND BLACKWATER POND

DAVID WILLIAM STRICKLEN

Copyright © 2007 by David William Stricklen.

ISBN: Hardcover   978-1-4257-6799-0
        Softcover   978-1-4257-6792-1

All rights reserved. No part of this book may be reproduced or transmitted in any form or by any means, electronic or mechanical, including photocopying, recording, or by any information storage and retrieval system, without permission in writing from the copyright owner.

This is a work of fiction. Names, characters, places and incidents either are the product of the author's imagination or are used fictitiously, and any resemblance to any actual persons, living or dead, events, or locales is entirely coincidental.

This book was printed in the United States of America.

To order additional copies of this book, contact:
Xlibris Corporation
1-888-795-4274
www.Xlibris.com
Orders@Xlibris.com
40432

Contents

Chapter One: The Incident 9

Chapter Two: Enter the Membrane 24

Chapter Three: New Arrival 40

Chapter Four: Exodus 57

Chapter Five: The Dangling 75

Chapter Six: The Party 88

Chapter Seven: A Taste of Infinity 101

Chapter Eight: Gerbits and Toadstools 109

Chapter Nine: The Winds End 124

Chapter Ten: Surprise Visit 139

A note from the author 157

First, a very special thanks to my wife, Cheryl, and my two sons, Justin and Jordan. My son Jordan read the story many times and told me that it was his favorite book. To know that makes it all worthwhile no matter what else happens.

My life long friend Robin Crossman was instrumental in getting my book on the Internet. She invested countless hours of her free time to make it happen.

Last but not least, thanks to my good friend, Dan Sharp. I have been friends with Dan since the second grade. He put his vast creative talents to work and drew the wonderful illustrations for the book.

Chapter One

The Incident

Brian Hummel woke up to a bright beam of sunlight hitting his face through an open window. The tall 16-year-old sat up, sleepy-eyed.

He could hear the sound of running feet approaching his door. The door crashed open with a bang and slapped against the wall. His little brother stood smiling in the doorway. Tommy was a small-boned 12-year-old with stringy blond hair and freckles splattered across his face.

"Morning Brian," he said with a smile.

"Mornin'," Brian mumbled.

"Better get up."

"What time is it?" Brian asked, flopping his long legs out of bed.

"I don't know, but Mom said if I didn't get you out of bed pretty soon, we'd have to eat lunch instead of breakfast."

"What's for lunch?" Brian grinned.

"Cereal," said Tommy, turning and walking back down the hall.

Brian picked the sleep from the corner of his eye. He put on a pair of old shorts and a black T-shirt with the sleeves cut off. He made his way down the hall trying to push his thick mass of dark curly hair into order with his fingers.

Pulling up a chair, he sat down to breakfast with his mother, brother, and grandmother. Grandmother was hunched over her bowl of steaming Cream of Wheat. On this hot July morning she wore a brown sweater over a blue flowered dress and a black shawl pulled tightly around her shoulders. Her mind was clouded with memories. In fact, she spent more time with her memories than she did anywhere else.

"Morning Gram!" said Brian. Grandma stared solemnly into her cup of coffee, stirring it carefully, totally unaware. She watched closely as the cream formed swirling shapes.

"Mother!" Mrs. Hummel said. Grandma looked up. "Brian was talking to you."

"Black spirits at the pond today," Grandma said sternly.

Tommy squirmed impatiently in his seat. "Hurry up, Brian, so we can go to the pond and swim."

"We've got all day," Brian grumbled.

"But the guys are probably already there."

Grandma meticulously straightened the black shawl around her shoulders. "You two stay away from that pond. It is a dark nest for evil. Today will be a dark day. Mark my word. I just saw it in the cream."

"Not this again!" said Mrs. Hummel. She filled two bowls with equal amounts of cereal and set them on the table. Her arm quaked while she tried to navigate a full gallon of milk over top of the bowl.

Grandma leaned forward and whispered, as if afraid of being overheard. "There are many stories better left untold about that pond. Why, some say it is bottomless . . . it just goes on and on; down, down, down!"

Tommy blurted, "Dave said that he heard voices by it once and no one was there!"

"If no one was there, then how did he hear it?" Brian laughed.

"Let's finish breakfast shall we?" said Mrs. Hummel. She was always trying to maintain an organized house. She was a person who liked order and felt there was a time and place for everything.

"I'll race ya to the pond, Brian!"

"I'm only half done with my cereal," Brian answered with this mouth full. Tommy laughed as milk dribbled down Brian's chin.

Mrs. Hummel shook her head. Then asked, "Is Joey Hasselback going to be there?"

Tommy looked down. "I don't know, Ma."

"Is he still teasing you about not having a father?"

"Not since Brian tossed him around," said Tommy.

Mrs. Hummel glared at Brian. Thinking this could be the beginning of an endless lecture; Brian smiled faintly at his mother.

"Come on Tom," he said. "We haven't got all day, have we?"

Tommy laughed and they sprang from their chairs and went crashing out the back door of the old farmhouse. Within moments they were running through the small barnyard and into the hayfield toward the pond.

"Brian," gasped Tommy as they leaped through the tall grass.

"Yeah?"

"I hope Joey isn't there." They slowed to a walk.

"He's a jerk, Tom," Brian panted. "It makes him feel big to tease you."

"What can I do about it?"

"Show him you aren't going to take it."

"Okay, I'll show him," Tommy muttered.

Brian put a reassuring arm on Tommy's shoulder. "It'll be okay, Tom. Don't even worry about him. I'll be there, and after all we came to have fun . . . right?"

Tommy smiled. "Right!"

Within minutes they arrived at the pond. It was small and eerie, enclosed by leafy bushes and monstrous twisted trees with vines dangling from their overhanging branches. In the center of the pond was a raft the boys had built a few summers before. It was a safe place for poor swimmers and the main attraction of the pond.

The four other guys had already been swimming when Tommy and Brian got there.

"Come on in you guys!" Dave called out. Brian tossed off his shirt and ran into the deep inviting water. Going under, he pushed himself along smoothly, gliding through the depths. His face bobbed up on the surface and he squirted a stream of water out of his mouth.

Tommy, meanwhile, tested the water with his toe and started to wade in. Joey Hasselback saw Tommy inching his way into deeper water. "Afraid to dive in, you sissy?" Tommy glared at Joey, and then continued his slow descent.

Brian floated on his back, staring up at the vines dangling over the water. He was awakened from his trance by a splash and a gasp as Joey erupted through the surface of the pond. "I did it, I touched bottom; I did it!" Joey yelled, choking on his words.

Chapter One

Brian frowned in disgust. "Aw, you did not!"

Joey paused. "I bet your baby brother can't do it!"

"Oh yeah?" said Tommy as he swam toward the raft.

"No one's ever touched bottom-it's too deep. Joey's lying," said Toby.

Tommy pulled himself up on the raft. "Well I can," he said.

"Forget it, Tom. Don't let Joey get to ya," said Brian.

"But I can do it," said Tommy, "even if Joey can't." Tommy stood dripping on the wobbly deck of the homemade raft. He sucked in deeply, absorbing all the air his small lungs could hold.

"Don't do it Tom," Brian said, climbing aboard the raft.

"Aw, he'll be okay," said Dave.

Lungs fully inflated, Tommy plunged straight down into the warm, dark water. They all leaned over the raft, staring in silence as they saw his feet trail off and slowly fade away.

A minute or so crept by, but Tommy had not resurfaced.

"He's been down there a long time," said Dave.

"Yeah, way too long," Brian nodded worriedly. "Look," he said, pointing into the depths. A small trail of blue bubbles approached the surface from far below.

"No!" Brian stammered in disbelief. He instinctively dove into the pond, clawing his way to the bottom following the small trail of bubbles his brother had left behind. Swimming frantically, he made his way down deep into the seemingly bottomless pond.

Brian felt a twinge of dizziness and knew that soon he would pass out from lack of air. Committed to saving his brother, he pushed even harder, propelling himself down into the cool darkness. As his lungs strained, blackness began to close in around his face.

Knowing he was fading beyond return, Brian stopped and looked toward the surface.

Silent echoes of his brother's voice beckoned him to continue. "Brian . . . Brian." Semi-conscious, he hesitated, then pushed himself upward to the shimmering sunlight.

He gasped and thrashed wildly as he broke through the surface. He felt someone grab his arms and pull him onto the raft.

"Did Tommy come up yet?" Brian coughed.

"No," one of the boys said. Brian struggled to his feet for another try, but was held back by his friends.

"Don't do it again," warned Dave. "You'll kill yourself."

Defeated, Brian sunk down to his knees and stared into the unfriendly water. "He's alive, I know it . . . I heard his voice. He was talking to me!" Brian, entranced, sat as silent tears slid down his face.

They stood quiet for a minute or two, and then sirens began to whine in the distance, gradually growing louder.

Joey Hassleback burst through the bushes. "I told your mom, Brian," he yelled, "and she called the police!"

Mrs. Hummel stumbled into the clearing and ran into the water. She thrashed her arms in agony. "Why? Why Tommy? . . . No please, not my Tom!"

The screaming sirens stopped and an eerie silence took their place. Police were running through the brush to the edge of the pond.

"Where did the boy go down?" asked the sergeant. Brian, shaking nervously on the raft, pointed out into the water.

"How long ago?"

"About ten minutes," replied Brian.

The sergeant looked down and sadly shook his head.

A crowd of chattering neighbors quickly began to gather.

"What happened?" asked one woman.

"Tommy Hummel drowned."

"Oh my God!" she exclaimed.

"I suggest that everyone go back to their homes," the sergeant said firmly.

Brian had swum ashore and was trying to comfort his mother. "He's alive Ma, I heard his voice."

"What?"

"I heard his voice calling to me when I went down after him." This news only upset her more as she stood on the bank, completely horrified.

The large policeman walked over to them. "Mrs. Hummel, why don't you take your son home?"

"But I want to take both of them home!" she cried.

"I'm sorry, but I think it will be best. I've called in a special rescue team to come out and drag the pond to find your son. I promise I'll let you know the minute I find out anything."

"No," she cried hysterically, "I won't leave until I find my son!"

"Ma'am, we're doing everything possible," the sergeant said gently. "I understand how you feel, but there's nothing here for you to do."

"All right," she quietly agreed, staring into the dark water. Clutching Brian, she started for home.

The rest of the day seemed to grind slowly by. Mrs. Hummel and Brian sat quietly in the living room gazing out the window. Grandma rocked slowly in her squeaky rocking chair, watching the two of them.

"I heard his voice," Brian said aloud.

Mrs. Hummel turned to Brian. "Did you swim all the way down to the bottom looking for him?"

Grandma snapped in sudden anger. "He couldn't have gone to the bottom! That pond goes straight down into hell!" Her words lingered like bad omens, and the quiet once again closed around Brian and his mother.

Lost in thought, Brian was startled by a dull thumping at the front door. "The policeman . . ." Brian blurted. Mrs. Hummel and Brian went to the door; Grandma rose slowly and hobbled behind them.

Brian opened the door and the sergeant stood grimly before them. They stared at him, weighing the rest of their lives on his every word.

He cleared his throat and began. "We've been combing the pond all day and couldn't find anything . . . not a trace."

"You checked the whole pond, all the way down to the bottom?" Brian asked.

"Yes we did, although that's not your average pond. It's incredibly deep at the center."

"Straight down into hell," Grandma croaked.

The sergeant looked at the old woman, then continued. "I called a geologist friend of mine, and he said the pond may have been formed by a meteorite thousands of years ago."

Grandma nodded as if this proved she was right.

"There's also a magnetic field near the bottom that gave our equipment some trouble. Regardless, we went over every inch of that bottom. No body, no nothing. Either the body vanished or . . ." he threw a penetrating glance at Brian, "someone isn't telling the whole story."

"I am! I swear he went down and didn't come up," Brian stammered.

"Very well," said the sergeant.

He turned to Mrs. Hummel, who stood frozen in the doorway, "Let me know if anything else strange happens around that pond or if your youngest son wanders home." The sergeant frowned slightly, and then returned to his vehicle.

"If Tommy isn't in the pond then where is he?" asked Brian.

Mrs. Hummel looked at her son, almost hoping he was playing some horrible trick. She knew he wasn't.

Three days had passed since Tommy's disappearance. Brian sat alone under an oak tree in the back yard. He plucked a blade of grass and stuck it in his mouth as he thought about his brother's bizarre disappearance.

"Brian," said a voice.

Brian looked up and saw Dave walking through the yard toward him. As usual Dave had on a stretched out T-shirt that hung on his slender frame. Dave took off his glasses and began to search for a clean spot on his shirt to wipe them off.

"Don't you have any chores today?" Dave asked, finding the bottom corner of his shirt.

"Mom started selling most of the animals today. She wants to move away from this place, Brian said"

Dave sat down next to him in the cool grass. "Running away won't help."

"I know," Brian muttered.

"How ya feeling?"

"Well . . . I'm okay, but you know, I just can't believe Tommy's dead. It feels like he's still around."

"What do you mean?"

"Okay, like just now," Brian, said. "When you walked up I heard a twig crack and for an instant I thought it was Tommy. I really think he's still alive . . . I can just feel it! They couldn't find his body you know."

"Ya, there's definitely something weird about that pond," Dave sighed.

"My grandma says it goes straight down into hell. Isn't that sick?"

Dave shook his head. "When my great uncle heard what happened to Tommy he came up with some weird old stories too."

"Oh yeah?"

"Yup." Dave continued, "He said when he was little the trees around the pond would whisper to him when the wind blew."

"What did the trees say?"

"I don't know, but he even remembers his grandpa telling him strange stories about it."

"I don't know what to think anymore." Brian said.

"You won't catch me swimming in there again! Everyone else is too creeped out to go back there too."

"I've got to find out what happened to Tommy," Brian said. "I miss him. He is my little brother."

"Brian!" called Mrs. Hummel, "where have you been? It's time to eat."

"See ya," said Brian.

"Bye."

Brian walked into the house and sat down at the kitchen table. He quietly toyed with his food.

"Why aren't you eating?" his mother asked.

"I'm not too hungry, Ma. It just seems so quiet without Tommy."

"Don't start! We can't be crying at the table every night."

"Yeah," Brian agreed.

Grandma, paying no attention, gummed her mashed potatoes.

"Mom, can I go down to the pond tomorrow?"

"Why?" she asked.

Grandma stopped chewing and took sudden interest in the conversation.

"Mom, there's something about that pond."

"What?"

"I don't know, it's weird . . . I think there must be some answers there."

Grandma interrupted. "Brian, there's an old rhyme we used to sing to each other when I was a little girl."

"How does it go?"

She spoke in her dry cracking voice. "Blackwater Pond is a dark nest for evil. There is something in the shadows taking the lives from our people. They must be used for some hellacious task because their spirits come alive when the wind whistles past."

"How creepy can you get!" said Brian.

Mrs. Hummel looked at Grandma who had already resumed eating. "Mother, I wish you would stop saying things like that. It bothers Brian."

"Doesn't bother me," he said.

"Well, it bothers me!" she shrieked.

Grandma concentrated on eating, unaware of what was happening around her. Mrs. Hummel stared and sighed, realizing the conversation had been pointless.

After supper Brian watched a little TV, then went to bed. He pulled the covers up snugly against his face.

His mind drifted through a sleepy haze to the pond and his brother's drowning. He saw himself diving into the pond, pushing deeper and deeper, strangled for air. He saw Tommy thrust out his hand from far below as an unknown force pulled him down.

"Brian!" he called out.

Brian reached for him, but Tommy slipped away vanishing into the depths. Tommy's voice echoed distantly in his mind.

He awoke with a start and sat straight up, eyes wide, face pale. He propped himself up with a pillow and leaned back taking a deep breath as he wiped the cool sweat from his forehead. He felt the crisp night air, brush against his damp face.

"I heard him calling out when I went down after him," Brian said to himself. "I know I did."

"Brian," whispered a voice from the outside.

"Who's there? Tommy is that you?"

Brian felt an icy chill come through the open window, billowing the curtains. Shivering, he pulled the covers up. His eyes darted around the dark room.

"Come to the pond," beckoned the voice.

Brian's voice wavered. "Where are you Tommy?"

"Come to the pond . . . help me . . ."

"You sound kind of funny."

"Come now," the voice murmured.

"Are you okay Tommy? Tommy!"

Brian felt the cold chill leave the room, sucking the curtains out the window with it. Then all was still and he knew he was once again alone.

Common sense told him not to go to the pond, but a combination of curiosity and love for his brother made it impossible for him to resist. He climbed quietly out of bed and got dressed, then slid through the open window into the darkness.

Brian went to the woodshed and took out his father's old lantern. He fumbled in the dark for matches, lit the lantern, and watched as it took on a tarnished yellow glow. The night was alive with crickets and frogs and other earthy things that sing in the darkness. A soft breeze was rustling the leaves and shadows danced from wind-tossed branches. Brian kept glancing behind him, thinking he felt the presence of another.

"I don't know if I should be doing this," he thought as he parted the tall grass and began to make his way to the pond. The moon stood like a ghostly beacon above the passing clouds. He had been to the pond hundreds of times, but in the night nothing looked familiar.

Slowly a lifeless silence began to close in on the field. All he could hear was the crackling of damp leaves under his bare feet and the hard thumping of his heart.

"Brian," whispered a lingering voice.

He stopped, straining to see through the wall of blackness surrounding him. He moved the lantern toward the voice.

"Who's there?" he gasped.

"You must hurry, hurry . . . now!"

Brian ran wildly through the moist grass. Stumbling and clawing, sweat dripping from his face, he neared the pond. He fell through a clump of bushes and landed face down on the dewy grass.

He looked up and before him was the pond, dark and lifeless, the moon reflecting off its glassy surface. A breeze blew up off the water and he thought he could hear whispers in the wind. Shadows from overhanging trees danced across the water. He got back to his feet and walked to the dark pool.

Brian felt the chill of a thousand eyes watching him, laughing at him.

"Enter the pond," said a breathy voice.

"Tommy, where are you?" What happened to you?" He began to wade in. The water was warm and murky.

"I'm down here, down deep," said the voice.

"How can you be down there?" he said in horror. Now the water up to his waist, he looked deep into the pond. He held up the lantern and saw fading images of his brother's face under the water.

"Is that you, Tom?"

Unfriendly whispers broke the stillness as the wind whistled through the trees. The whispers gradually grew louder and louder into taunting screams.

Suddenly Brian heard a blood-curdling scream.

"Save me Brian!"

Brian dove into the tarnished water and swam out toward the image he had seen. Blinded by darkness Brian submerged, searching but not knowing what he'd find.

A current began to spin around him, pulling him down into the unknown depths. He struggled wildly, but the force of the whirlpool overpowered him.

He heard silent echoes of Tommy's voice calling to him. "Swim for the hole!"

Brian felt himself tiring. Straining for air, he fought helplessly for the surface. The current was merciless, sucking him down.

Exhausted, head spinning, blackness closed in around him. His fear began to fade, as he slid out of consciousness.

Brian no longer worried about what was happening. Peace and total calm had seeped into him. He felt he was drifting free from the confines of his body, then all faded to black . . .

Chapter Two
Enter the Membrane

    Brian stirred, his consciousness lazily coming back to him. He opened his eyes slowly. In front of him was a glistening pool of water.

"Am I looking down on it or up at it," he wondered. "Am I dead? I don't feel dead. But then I don't know what dead feels like." He brought his hands up in front of his face and examined them. "I still look the same." He patted down his body, feeling for his legs. "Everything's here," he said aloud. His voice repeated in deep resonating echoes.

Brian felt the ground next to him and realized he was lying on his back, not floating in the air. He took a deep breath to clear his head and sat up to get some idea of where he was. He found he was sitting alone in a dark winding tunnel. The walls and floor were covered with monstrous tree roots and damp moss. Overhead was a circular opening with water suspended across it.

"That must be where I came in. I must be under the pond! It's so strange how the water just hangs there." He stood up to inspect it more closely. Brian swirled his hand in the pool overhead and discovered it was wet. He moved his face closer to get a good look. He became mesmerized as he watched the grass swaying gently on the bottom of the pond and a school of minnows swimming by. "What is this place? This is amazing. I . . . I can't believe this!"

Tommy must be alive; he has to be down here somewhere. "Tommy!" his voice echoed.

Brian made his way down the tunnel, feet squishing in the cool moss. "I wonder how many people have come this way? I guess all those old stories were true. They were always about people disappearing." Brian frowned "I never heard about anyone ever coming back."

The tunnel twisted in all directions as if it were dug by a giant worm. "What's this?" Brian noticed a small moss covered object. He reached down and picked it up. It was a child's doll stinking with decay. "A child's doll?" He rubbed his thumb on the head and exposed a white porcelain face. "Weird, this doll must have been down here for a long, long time," he said aloud, his voice resonating. The fabric arms began to fall apart as he gently laid the doll back down. As he moved further along, it gradually began getting lighter. He rounded a bend and came upon a clear thick membrane sealing off the entrance to the tunnel. He looked into it and saw fuzzy colored images on the other side. Timidly he pushed against it. It was cold to the touch and jiggled like a bowl of Jell-O. On impulse, he pushed his whole arm through. The Jell-O-like substance closed cold and snug around Brian's arm. He could feel a warm breeze touching his outstretched fingertips on the other side.

"This had to be the way Tommy went," he thought.

Brian began to step through the membrane. It clung to him, stretching as he pulled toward the other side. It felt like rubber cement sticking to and pulling on his hair and skin. When he was through, it snapped back into place, jiggling for a moment.

Brian looked around curiously. He was in a thick green forest of strange trees. Their giant winding trunks were covered with leafy vines. The forest floor was brush and soft grass. He glanced back at the membrane and the tunnel. "It looks more like a cave now," he thought. Brian looked up and saw sunlight cutting through the trees. "How can I be under the pond?" Angry-looking orange clouds with a sunlit crimson tint hovered overhead. "Am I dead?"

The wind picked up and a shallow voice whispered hauntingly, "You are alive."

"Who are you? Are you the voice that led me here?"

"I am like the wind, I can be felt but not held, heard but not seen."

"Where am I?" Brian asked. He pushed against the membrane to make sure he could return. It gave a little, but his hand would not penetrate.

He heard twigs crack and strange voices. Frantically he pushed on the membrane but could not get back through. He heard the sound of someone running rapidly toward him.

Brian turned and saw three strange humanoids charging at him. They were all close to five foot tall, stocky, and dressed in glistening black armor. Their armor was covered with small spikes and a separate row of huge spikes ran down their backs. They were bearing giant swords that stood nearly as tall as they did.

"This is crazy," Brian thought, instinctively taking up a defensive stance.

"A Thork!" yelled the fat knight as he ran toward Brian. Brian scrambled for a branch under a tree but the fat knight was already on him and moving in for the kill. Then the knight stumbled on a vine and tripped forward.

Brian brought the branch off the ground and into the knight's helmet, sending him tumbling backward.

The knight's dented helmet toppled off revealing a pudgy, pushed-in face. A second knight grunted, taking a full swing at Brian's head. Brian ducked as the sword whistled a few inches over his back, slicing through a small tree and toppling it to the ground. Brian picked the pudgy knight's sword off the forest floor and ran to the membrane. He slashed at it, but the sword bounced off. The knights then descended upon him. Thrusting their swords into Brian's face. He let his sword fall free. The fat knight was still lying on his back, clutching his throbbing head.

"Kill the non-believer," he growled as he stood up.

"Hey Pug! He's funny looking like the other one."

"The other one??" said Brian.

"Ya, thin, same accent too."

"Tommy . . . you must have Tommy."

"Kill the non-believer," barked the fat knight.

"No! We'll take this one to the castle for King Bara. He likes odd ones like this for sacrifice and it's rare we get to sacrifice a matched set."

"Were you surprised to see us, non-believer?"

"Nothing surprises me anymore," Brian replied. "Where am I?"

"You're in trouble, you dim scrud!"

"I swear they get dumber and uglier all the time."

Brian frowned and began looking for some way to escape, but with a knight on each arm and a sword pushing into his back, they took him away.

"You speak English? Who are you guys?" Brian asked. They all laughed. The fat one glanced at his comrade and said, "Chucklehead."

"Don't you know it! Could he be from over the mountain?"

"Maybe he's mad!" The pudgy knight turned and looked Brian in the eye. "We're taking you to the castle for sacrifice. Now shut up!

There is nothing worse then a prisoner that doesn't know when to stop talking. Keep moving!"

When they reached the edge of the forest, Brian saw a castle in the distance. It was ghastly, with ancient dark walls twisting upward. It sat on the side of a jagged mountain across a deep valley of tall grass. They made their way down the hill and into the valley.

Suddenly they heard whoops and war cries from behind. They turned and saw hoards of men in robes the color of red clay crashing out of the forest and careening down the valley at them.

"Nimbus will protect us," said the dark knight, placing his sword in front of him.

"Non-believers must die!" said another as the flood of rebels closed in.

Brian felt the knight's grasp loosening and jerked his arm free of the vice-like grip. He saw a sword coming around as he leapt to freedom, but not before the icy blade cut deeply across his back. Stumbling, then regaining his balance, he ran for safety. The clash of steel and cries of pain faded into the distance. Brian ran until his breath drowned out the sounds, and then he ran some more. He could feel the warm blood running down his back and as the blood drained, so did his strength.

He collapsed, exhausted, into the grass at the top of a hill. He tied his shirt around his chest, to stop the bleeding from the wound. From a safe distance he watched the angry clash of swords and pain exchanged between the stocky beings.

After a time, Brian sat up weakly and pondered his next move. "I must get back through the membrane somehow," he thought. "I could go back and get help, if anyone believed me, then we could come back and get Tommy out of the castle before they kill him. Which way was it to the membrane?" Brian staggered to his feet and saw a thick forest off in the distance. He noticed that mountains surrounded the valley and forest on all sides.

The sun was setting off in the distance and splotches of orangish red clouds were hanging overhead like vultures. Stumbling and struggling with each step, Brian made his way into the forest. Everything looked dark and mysterious. Slowly he pawed his way through the trees.

"I'll never find the membrane," he gasped. "I'll have to stay here and figure out some way to save Tommy myself. These little tough guys speak English, maybe they were taught by other people who were trapped here."

As the evening wore on, Brian became frightened of strange animal noises he had never heard before. "I'm so helpless." He felt his confidence draining. "No! I can't give up. I must be strong . . ." He took a deep breath, trying to regain some of his lost strength, but he could feel the cut burning across his back and knew he was teetering on the edge of exhaustion.

Brian stared at the stars as a breeze cooled his damp face. None of the stars seemed to be in the right place and many looked too bright. Two warm blue moons were shining down on him. "This part of the woods isn't bad," he thought. "But it still kinda gives me the creeps!"

With his next step the earth beneath his feet gave way. Brian tumbled through a camouflaged trap door in the forest floor and in the next instant was sliding down a long winding tube. He rolled from side to side as he shot downward. He could see he was going to hit something blocking the end. A solid thud sounded as his feet slammed into a round wooden door.

Brian could hear gruff voices coming from the other side. White light pierced through the splintered boards. The door jerked open and he spilled out onto a floor of soft moss. He was instantly surrounded by a group of short, stocky beings. "Have you come to join us?" one of them asked.

"No," Brian muttered in confusion. Spears were suddenly thrust at him.

"He's a Tred spy!" said a squeaky voice from the back.

Brian looked up, his eyes cloudy. "I don't know what you mean."

An older being with a long gray beard and a reddish brown robe pushed his way through the crowd to Brian. He stood over him and scratched his head slowly, as if to think.

"He must be one of King Bara's Black Knights," said one.

Another poked Brian in the side with a stick and bellowed, "Let's chop out his gizzard and feed it to the lizard." They all chuckled.

The bearded old man waved his hand angrily. "He's no Tred, you mossbacks. Look how tall and skinny he is. You came from over the crest of the mountains, didn't you son?" Brian nodded in bewilderment. "Any questions tall one?"

"When do I wake up?" asked Brian.

The old man smiled and said, "Welcome . . . name's Slizard. I run the whole show down here."

Brian's eyelids closed and the voices were growing dimmer. Within moments, he lost consciousness.

"Get the vat ready for this one," said Slizard, pointing at two of his men.

The next day Brian woke to find a strange being staring into his face with crazed eyes and open mouth. Brian was sitting in a tub of hot bubbling yellow fluid. He felt energized. The wound, which had burned across his back, was but a faint memory.

"Pleased to meet your humblest of acquaintance," said the being. "The name's Ebil J. Yabut." He stuck out his hand. Instead of shaking it, Brian looked down at the bubbling fluid with puzzlement. "Don't worry, we aren't having you for lunch. You're just the spike in the punch," said the creature.

"What?" asked Brian as he stared at the golden bubbles rising from the bottom of the tub.

"My son, the hands of fate will never know what lies in store for you, Black Crow."

"Did you call me Black Crow? My name is Brian."

Slizard rose and walked over to them. He put his hand on Ebil's shoulder and grinned at Brian.

"He's quite mad, you know" Slizard said. Ebil began making faces by pushing in his nose. "And very dangerous," he added.

"Hay, nonny, nonny . . . nonny," Ebil sang, revealing his broken yellow teeth.

"Why do you keep him around?" Brian asked.

"Good luck, you know," Slizard smiled. "What do we call you?"

"Raven," interrupted Ebil. Brian glared at Ebil and made his best monster face.

"My name is Brian!"

Ebil stepped back and looked at him out of the corners of his eyes. "You swooped into this world like a Raven."

"More like a fish," Brian replied. Ebil began laughing wildly.

Slizard pushed Ebil back saying, "Leave him be. Find something better to do!" Offended, Ebil frowned, looked down at his shoes and shuffled away.

"Why am I sitting in this hot goo?" Brian asked.

"It will rejuvenate you. You were bleeding pretty badly when we got you. Your body is absorbing this fluid. It'll make you strong as ten Gerbits."

Brian looked puzzled. "What's a Gerbit?"

Slizard laughed. "I'm sorry! There's much I must tell you if you plan to survive."

"I do!"

"Well," Slizard began, "first, let me tell you about us Thorks. One hundred eighty some years ago Thorks roamed the horizons looking for a place to live that was as peaceful as they were. They found this place, the valley of tears. It was surrounded by mountains on all sides."

Brian leaned forward in interest. "The name alone doesn't sound too encouraging."

Slizard nodded "They felt this would be a good home because the mountain range would protect them against large gargons and other beasts. The beasts were too large to climb the mountain and make it down the narrow paths. Once in a while, however, a beast would make the climb, and devour some. A huge castle was built in the side of the mountain for protection. Sixteen years ago a Trediarian ruler, Bara, from a land across the Steam Sea, was on a Nimbian crusade. He found our castle and desired it for his own. He took the castle by force while we were asleep. A handful of men and myself escaped and since then have been hiding under the forest floor. They try even now to seek us out and kill us under the orders of their ruler, King Bara."

"Why?"

"He tells them the red clouds are gods. His people must believe and respect what he says. They refer to the clouds as God Nimbus. According to him, our men must die because we don't believe. But we ambush his patrols and have slim hopes of one day regaining what should be ours."

"He sounds like a dangerous guy," said Brian. "Are you a king?"

"My father was when we had the castle," said Slizard, "but he was very old and died in the attack. The throne was passed to me and now I'm the king of this mole hole."

Brian glanced around. It was a homey place they had constructed underground. The room was large and round. Small tunnels branched off from the main room in all directions. In front of him was a roaring fireplace in a hearth shaped like an open mouth. The floor was soft moss. The room was full of earthy looking tables and chairs with Thorks moving about.

"Where does the smoke go from the fire?" Asked Brian.

"It fills a connecting tunnel to keep intruders away."

"Oh."

Slizard heard someone coming behind him. "Well, Razz. What brings you to this?"

"What's this Tred spy doing boiling in our finest fluids?"

"He's no spy. He's a boy that's come from another place, from over the crest of the horizon. Aren't you, son?" Brian quickly nodded. Razz frowned, rolling his eyes.

"You mean to tell me that this boy traveled all that way by himself without being devoured by gargons? Sorry Sliz, but I just can't buy it. You've been seeing too many moon-struck wizards lately."

Slizard reddened. Brian sat still, not saying a word. Slizard barked back at Razz gruffly, "You're the chuckle-head, you noodle-witted krouton. Can't you see how long and thin he is? He's not from around here."

Razz' mind was racing trying to think of a reply because he knew he was losing the argument. "Why, he's just some kind of freak, an elongated abnormality."

Brian frowned at this remark.

A Thork ran into the room panting. "Black knights are in the valley!"

The next moment was total chaos. Thorks ran in different directions, grabbing clubs, spears, and oversized swords that were leaning against the walls.

Slizard rushed off and Razz turned to Brian in the midst of the mania. "To prove on which side you stand, you will lead the charge today!"

"Wonderful," said Brian sarcastically.

Razz grabbed Brian and jerked him from the tub. He hit Brian in the face with a towel and ordered, "Dry yourself off, then put this on!" He tossed him a baggy robe. "Hurry!" yelled Razz as he threw on a robe of his own and snatched up a sword.

Slizard ran over to Razz. "What's he doing with the robe on?"

Razz smiled. "He volunteered to lead the charge today to prove he's worthy."

"Very well!" Slizard replied with excitement.

Brian scowled as he tied the robe.

"I'll go get you my biggest, finest sword!" Slizard said as he ran toward one of the tunnels.

"Wait a minute," stammered Razz. "All the new men get clubs."

"I'm in command down here. Now go above with the rest." Slizard returned from the tunnel with a gleaming sword. He held it out in his hands. "This is now yours."

Brian looked at its bulk. "I can't swing that!"

"What does 'can't' mean?" questioned Slizard.

Brian was ashamed that he had given up before he even started. "It's just a word losers use where I come from." Brian reached forward, palms sweaty, and slowly pulled the sword from Slizard's grasp with both hands on the grip. He waited for the sword's tremendous weight to shift to its new bearer. Slizard let go, but nothing happened. It didn't fall to the ground. It seemed to float weightlessly in the air.

"Boy, is this light!"

Slizard grinned and nodded.

Brian began slashing it about, cutting through the air at imaginary attackers. Slizard stepped back with a wide grin. "You'll do just fine, son. You can swing that sword faster than anything I've ever seen. The Black Knights will be much stronger, but you are much quicker. Yes, you'll do just fine." Brian smiled at this encouragement and laid the sword on his shoulder like he had seen the others do.

The tunnels were emptying and everyone was scrambling above. "We must go now," croaked Slizard as he grabbed a sword of his own from over the fireplace.

Slizard wore a long, clay-red robe with two black bands on the right arm that distinguished him from the others.

Brian looked at Slizard's arm as they moved through the tunnel. "Are those two bands for bravery or something?"

"No. One's for wisdom and the other is for depth of thought," answered Slizard. "Someday I'd like to earn another for consideration, but there's no chance of that while we're in a battle, is there?"

They approached the middle of a tunnel where a ladder made of roots was built into a wall. It went straight up to the surface.

"This way," said Slizard as he grabbed the lower rung and began his ascent. They emerged through a disguised trap door that was surrounded by large leafy bushes and ferns.

Brian could hear the hum of whispering voices. There were forty or fifty Thork warriors with an assortment of spears, clubs, and swords. Brian saw Razz pointing through the trees on the edge of the forest. Down in the valley of tall grass was a patrol of about thirty Tred Knights. The sun glistened off their swords and polished black armor.

"Come, time is tight," urged Slizard as he rapped Brian on the shoulder. Brian snapped out of his daze and followed Slizard over to where Razz stood.

He felt the electric twinge of excitement and fear. His limbs began to feel limp and he became conscious of his breathing.

"Are you ready?" asked Razz.

Brian gulped, his throat cracking with dryness. "Uh, yeah."

"When I say go," Slizard said, "we'll all run right behind you." Brian nodded, staring at the ground. His stomach was churning and his hands were sweating, making the sword grip slippery. He shivered and goose bumps rose on his skin while he perspired. Running the other way entered his mind, but he decided that would be even more dangerous.

"Now!" shouted Razz. Brian jumped out of his skin. Slizard gave him a fatherly push down the incline into the valley. He stumbled forward and in the next moment was sprinting into the valley. Everyone was letting loose with hideous screams. Brian looked back. They all had their swords raised, so Brian turned and did the same. He tried yelling like the rest of them, but his heart wasn't in it. They were closing in on the Tred warriors.

"I will be injured," Brian thought. "But I'll fight 'em with all I have . . . to live."

The wind began to whistle and a voice whispered, "keep one eye on the knights and one eye on the sky or you will die!" The wind slowed down as the words faded.

He glanced up and saw a large mass of reddish-orange clouds speeding in their direction from the distance. No one else seemed to notice.

The Black Knights were lined up in two "v" formations, one behind the other, facing their attackers with swords in the air. When the command was given, they dropped their swords to waist-high, pointing straight out, and stomped toward the charge with fearless confidence.

The impact would be any moment. It seemed suicidal to run into a row of swords. Brian tried to slow down but he kept getting pushed from behind. He gripped his sword tightly and brought it back like a baseball bat.

His conscious mind left his body, at that moment. All the yelling and fear seemed so far away as his mind drifted, dreaming of distant things. "I must concentrate," he thought to himself.

As Brian ran into the row of swords, his mind faithfully returned. He gave a hard glancing blow, knocking the swords to the side and away from his belly. His momentum carried him crashing into one of the knights. The sharp spikes on the knight's armor pierced his skin as they collided. The knight and Brian went down together, tumbling backwards into the tall grasses. Brian looked around, and saw a forest of moving legs and clanging swords surrounding him. He glanced up in time to see a Black Knight preparing to split him in two. There was no time to react. Brian, in one last useless effort, attempted to reach for his sword as the knight's blade came down. Crack! Across the face of the attacker slashed a sword. The knight fell backwards, clasping his face. Brian sat up to see his savior. "Ebil!"

"Mind if I join you?" Ebil said, sitting down next to Brian casually, as if on a quiet picnic.

"You saved my life!" Brian yelped, taking his sword and rising to his feet.

"It is much better to be alive," replied Ebil.

Brian looked at the confusion and chaos around him and tried to defend himself. A knight came storming at him in a crazed rage. As the knight raised his sword to strike, Brian blasted him across the chest. The knight buckled over as Brian came down with a blow to the shoulder. With deep dents in his armor, the warrior fell to the ground moaning. Brian moved through the crowd, swinging his sword to and fro and knocking knights out of the way and to the ground before they could react.

Recalling the words in the wind, Brian looked at the sky. The vulturous orange clouds were directly overhead and were moving low to the ground. Everyone was so involved with staying alive they didn't see them.

A gooey orange blob began to drip from the cloud. It appeared rubbery as the sun flashed off its glassy surface. The blob made a sliding descent staying connected to the cloud. Landing on one of Slizard's men like a spider, it enveloped the shocked victim. Brian watched in horror as the man tried to squirm out of the gooey blob that pulled him back into the cloud.

Thorks began screaming and running, but the Tred knights remained. Brian stood motionless for a moment, trying to digest what he had seen. The knights were cheering and thrusting their swords in the air. "God Nimbus has saved us!" yelled a knight, waving his sword in victory.

At that moment an orange blob dropped on the knight and lifted him away. The knights too began to scatter, and Brian wisely chose to do the same. Lingering screams of agony echoed behind him as the cloud let go with drips diving down on their prey. Running in panic, warriors tried to escape this real-life nightmare. Brian, running as fast as he could, was caught in a stampede of fleeing warriors.

Brian glanced up and saw a blob dropping down above him. He dove to get clear but the blob caught hold of his foot. It was icy cold and he felt his foot quickly go numb.

He kicked and pulled but the blob held fast. Still connected to the cloud by a thin strand, the blob lifted off the ground and began rising toward the cloud. Brian dangled under the blob by one foot. He gripped his sword with both hands and swung himself up, slicing through the jelly blob and cutting his foot free.

Brian fell into the soft grass with a thud and felt the wind rush out of his chest. He lay stunned for a moment, then kicked the orange goo off his foot and started running toward the forest. "That cloud has to be some kind of living organism," he thought.

Thunder rumbled, then the sky opened up with a crackling display of lightning. Rain came down with such force that it drenched everything instantly. The rain felt cool and clean, washing the sweat and grit from his face. When Brian reached the forest, he sat under a tree for a while to rest and watched the rain as it began to fill the Valley of Tears with water.

The sound of the rain hitting the leaves was soothing. "Brian!" yelled Razz. "Come in out of the rain, my boy!" Brian stood up and

Razz put his hand on Brian's shoulder. "You know, Brian, we had taken you for dead."

"Were you out looking for me?" Brian asked.

"Yeah, Sliz sent me." They walked back toward the tunnel. Razz looked at Brian feeling somewhat ashamed. "I'm sorry Brian, I was all wrong about you as I tend to be sometimes."

Brian smiled warmly then said, "I didn't know those clouds ate people. It almost got me. I was lifted away by my foot until I cut myself free."

"Really? Wow, I never saw anyone get free before. You're all right kid! Better wipe the goo off your foot though; it will eat right through those funny looking feet of yours." Brian knelt down and aggressively rubbed a handful of leaves on his foot. "You see, the clouds are carnivorous. They're part of what this battle is all about. The Tredarians worship them. They call them Nimbus. They believe if they give sacrifice to Nimbus it will protect them. They believe if you think differently than them, like us, you are a weed and must be plucked from the garden of life."

"Well then, how do they explain the knights being eaten too?"

"It's like this Brian. If a knight gets eaten, they probably say something like 'he must not have truly believed and we are thankful to Nimbus for weeding him out!'"

"They're hard to understand," said Brian.

Razz bent over and opened the tunnel door. "Come, let's get below. Oh, there's one more thing I want to say. You fought like a herd of snorting Gerbits today. You should be proud." Brian grinned and they both jumped in the tunnel and slid down to the security below.

Chapter Three

New Arrival

When Brian got below there was a big celebration going on. Thorks were laughing and drinking yellow syrup from large brown pots planted in the wall.

Slizard walked up behind Brian, slapping him on the back with a start. "Well, it's nice to see you're in good health."

"I just hope Tommy is," Brian replied.

"Tommy?"

"Yeah, he's my younger brother. I think he's been captured by those Black Knight guys."

"Oh my!" Slizard said scratching his gray head. "They will most certainly feed him to Nimbus. But there just might be a way to get him out."

"What is that?" stammered Brian.

"Uh . . . I don't know but . . . there just might be a way. I'll think on it."

As Slizard scratched, long gray hairs fell from his head and floated like feathers to the ground.

"Come," said Slizard, walking toward one of the tunnels branching off from the main room. "If you want to stay here you should learn your way around." They walked into the small tunnel, laughter and party noises fading. The tunnel was lit with torches lining the walls. They walked together slowly, casting flickering shadows. Every time Slizard spoke, his voice repeated in deep vibrating echoes. "This room to the right," he said, tapping on the door, "is where we keep prisoners or nasty animals. We had a dwarf Gargon in there once," he said.

"Gargon?" said Brian.

"Oh yeah; the woods on the other side of the mountains are full of 'em. No one ever goes back there though."

"Why not?" Brian asked.

"Because the woods are full of Gargons!"

Brian nodded.

"You see," Slizard said, "the Treds lived over the crest of the horizon a long time ago. They developed armor to help protect them against Gargons and other evil beasts. Then they discovered our castle protected by walls and mountains. They wanted it, you see . . . sooo one night they tried to chop us into little pieces."

"I've heard the story," said Brian.

"Oh," said Slizard, embarrassed.

"Do you have a tunnel that goes up under a pond?" Brian asked.

"No, but we have this one." Slizard pointed up through a hole in the tunnel ceiling. "It goes up inside a tree."

"What's it for?"

"It's our lookout. I'll show you." Slizard put his wrinkled hand on the bottom of a root ladder.

"Slizard!" echoed a voice. A small being stood in the shadows at the other end of the tunnel.

"Yes!"

"A knight has been spotted. There may be more."

"Very well! Brian, I've got to go now but there's no reason why you can't look around."

"Okay," said Brian, "I will."

Slizard hurried off and Brian climbed up the rungs inside the tree. It made Brian feel good to think that if there were trouble with Black Knights he would be left out of it and remain safely hidden.

He climbed up to a round opening over a large branch far above the forest floor. It was dark now. The cool rain quietly splattering against the branch entranced Brian.

Lightning flashed and lit up the forest. "What's that over there?" he thought, seeing a dark shape. He leaned over the limb, getting his head wet.

He could see a lone Black Knight wandering aimlessly through the forest. He watched as the Knight slashed at clumps of bushes with his sword, as he stumbled along. There was a loud clap of thunder and a blaze of lightning hit a tree in the forest with a deep echoing boom!

Then the Knight vanished into the ground. "He fell through the trap door!" Brian thought. He climbed down the ladder and ran through the tunnel into the main room.

When he arrived all the Thorks were standing by the round wooden door.

Razz grasped the handle. "I wonder what we got?"

"A Knight! I saw him fall when I was in the tree." said Brian.

Razz smiled and brushed back a few onlookers with his sword. Razz glanced back momentarily, then jerked open the door.

The Knight spilled out, stumbling while swinging his sword. Clubs connected rapidly to his head and torso. The Knight swung wildly, tripping over his own feet. Losing his bearing as he was knocked this way and that, he spun around and fell backwards over a chair, crashing to the ground unconscious. The Thorks stood around him admiring the fine dents they had made in his armor.

"He looks like a gargon tripped over him," said one Thork. They all chuckled.

"This big dent right here," said Razz pointing to the side of his head. "That's one of mine."

"Oooh well; see that one there," said another, "That's mine."

"No, that was mine!"

Slizard rapped a club on the table. All the clatter stopped as everyone's attention turned to him. "What's the matter Sliz?" Razz asked.

"Put him on the table over here so we can get a look at this doof."

The knight was hoisted and dropped on the table as Slizard had requested.

Everyone crowded around the table trying to see. Slizard was directly overhead inching the crumpled helmet off.

"Just give it a big yank, Sliz," yelled Razz.

"Have patience Razz," said Slizard. He gave it a little twist and then the helmet slid free, exposing the gentle face of a young girl. She was soft and pretty with flowing black hair that glistened with each flicker of the torches. Brian smiled warmly. Everyone was stunned. "A girl?" some said. Others oooh'd and ahhh'd, and still others stared in amazement.

"But, but, that doesn't make any sense," stammered Razz.

"It makes a little," answered Slizard. "It explains why he was so clumsy. He is a she, and the armor didn't fit. It was too bulky and heavy for her." Slizard raised her eyelid and looked into one eye.

Razz frowned at Slizard. "I mean, what's a girl doing stumbling through the forest in the pouring rain?"

"Clubbing bushes," Brian added.

Ebil edged closer to where the girl lay and grasped a big clump of her shiny black hair in his knobby fingers. He stared directly into Brian's eyes. Uncomfortably close to Brian's face, he spoke with eyes wide and mouth contorted. "We've got her in our web, but shall we spare this bumble? It has to bee!"

"Get outta my face and leave her alone!" said Brian, gritting his teeth and flexing his eyebrows, in hopes this would have some strange effect on the madman. Ebil grinned and shuffled away.

"Does anyone understand him?" Brian asked.

"Why should we?" Slizard asked.

"Get this wet armor off her before she rusts, then put her in a cell," Slizard said mildly.

"You heard 'em!" bellowed Razz, "Let's go!" With that the girl was lifted and carried away.

"What are you gonna do with her?" asked Brian.

"Kill her!" yelled Razz from across the room.

"No, no," said Slizard "We'll have to question her first, then I don't know."

Chapter Three

"Could I talk to her first? I'll stay with her and I'll talk to her right when she wakes up. Maybe I can find out something about my brother."

"Well . . . okay," said Slizard, "but be careful."

The Thorks dressed her in a robe, then carried her into a small warm room. It had piles of hay on the floor and a few barrels lying about. She was tossed carelessly into a big pile of hay. Brian walked in behind her and the heavy wooden door slammed behind them.

"Uh . . . don't forget to let me out!" Brian yelled.

Razz reopened the door and tossed in a large rusty key. "Here Brian, you can let yourself out," he said, then closed the door.

Brian picked up the key, and sat down on a barrel next to the girl. Rain pattered on the ground above as he relaxed and studied her face. A torch burned on the wall and he watched how the light danced smoothly across her delicate features. Despite being clad in a man's dirty robe she looked feminine. A blue sapphire necklace was the only piece of jewelry she wore. He could see softness and warmth. He just knew she must be shy, sweet and caring.

After several hours of patiently waiting, she began to wake up. Rolling over on the soft hay bed, she rubbed her sore muscles.

Brian smiled.

When she opened her dark brown eyes, she discovered she was a prisoner. Her memory came back with a snap.

Brian leaned forward and began to speak. "Uh . . . , I'm Bri . . ." Before he could finish she sprang off the ground like a leopard, lunging for his throat with both hands.

Brian grabbed her arms as they both fell backward over a barrel and into the hay. She thrashed and kicked wildly. Brian tried to contain her flying elbows without hurting her. He stood up, lifting her kicking, grunting body with him. Off balance, they both stumbled into the wooden door, Brian's back taking the full force of the blow. She tried to bite him as he took her down into the hay and knelt on her arms. Exhausted, she stopped struggling and began to cry.

Brian stared at her, trying to make sense of her actions. "What's the matter with you?" he asked.

"Don't kill me!" she pleaded, tears streaming down her face.

"Are you mental. Why would I kill you?"

"You're a Thork, a demented killer, you torture people and burn them."

"No! We don't . . . I don't think," said Brian.

"Well, I know you tie them up and pull out their toenails," she said confidently.

"No . . . Well, not that I've heard."

"My father says all Thorks are sadistic madmen."

"I've only met one madman," said Brian.

She became angry. "My father is King Bara! He tells all."

"Your father is Bara the King?"

"Yes," she answered with pride.

"Can I ask you something?" said Brian.

"As soon as you get off me!"

Brian got up and sat back on the barrel. The girl sat up and straightened her hair. "First, what's your name?"

"Cassie . . . Cassie Bara."

"Mine's Brian. What were you doing stumbling through the forest in the rain clubbing bushes?"

She looked down, the torches casting moving shadows on the wall. She took a deep breath, arranged her thoughts and began. "You see, my mother died as a result of my birth."

"She died in childbirth?" said Brian.

"Yes, and ever since I can remember my father has blamed me for it. When she died, my father took our people away to find a placed unmarked by misery. He found the castle. He knew it must be meant for our people. He says I am a constant reminder of my mother's death. He hates me."

"That doesn't explain why you're running around in the rain," said Brian.

"Give me a chance and I'll tell you! I thought that maybe if I could capture a Thork, maybe even Slizard himself and bring him back for sacrifice, my father would be proud of me."

"Oh sure," thought Brian.

"Are you laughing at me?" she barked.

"No," Brian quickly responded.

She cleared her thoughts and continued. "So I got into some old armor and snuck in with the patrol. When the fighting started it got to be too much. I ran into the woods and then I couldn't find my way out."

"Why were you clubbing the bushes?"

"My father told me that's where Thorks hide."

"Maybe you shouldn't listen to your father!"

She started sobbing again. "Do you know what he calls me?"

"What's that," Brian asked, leaning forward.

"Black witch," she burst out.

Brian frowned. "This story is weird." Cassie stood up and glared at him in anger. "I'm sorry," he said. "It wasn't what I was expecting you to say . . . black witch . . . how strange can you get!"

She put her hands on her hips. "I'm not going to tell you anymore. I should have known better than to talk to a Thork scrud like you!"

"No I'm sorry, really!" Brian said, hoping she saw that he meant it.

They both sat motionless as silence closed in around them. All they heard was the quiet crackling of flames and rain hitting the leaves above. Brian broke the silence. "You worship those red clouds, don't you?"

"Well, what's wrong with that?"

"You also offer human sacrifices."

"So?" she responded.

"Well," Brian continued, "my little brother Tommy has been captured and I'm afraid they're going to feed him to your red cloud. That is, if it hasn't happened yet."

"Sacrifice isn't for two days," she answered.

"I've got to get him out!"

Cassie sat thinking. "Maybe we can make some kind of deal."

"What kind of deal?"

She looked smug. "I take you back to the castle as my prisoner."

"No way!" grumbled Brian.

She continued. "I'll make sure you're put in the cell with your brother. It will please my father to see I have a captive, and then before sacrifice I'll sneak in and let you both out."

"Gee, I don't know."

"I give my word as a Trediarian and it's the only way you're going to save your brother," she stated.

"How about this." said Brian, "I let you out of this cell and in return you let Tommy out of his."

"No deal! My way or no way!" she said firmly.

Brian scowled. "I should know better, but I guess I don't have any other choices."

"Fine," she smiled, standing up and brushing herself off. "When do we leave?"

"Uh, I don't even know if it will be okay. I'll have to talk it over with Slizard first." Brian got up and headed for the door. "I'll be back shortly." He stepped out, locking the door with the rusty key. "Slizard's gonna love this," he said to himself as he walked toward the main room.

He found most of the Thorks laying on tables or the soft moss floor either snoring or belching. Empty mugs were scattered everywhere.

"Must have been some party," he thought out loud. He walked over to Slizard who lay face down on a table with his head and arms dangling over the edge. Brian got down on his knees and looked up at Slizard's dangling head. "Slizard?" Slizard continued to snore. "Sliz?"

"Snort, wha, what? Brrriian. I'm supposed to be wise, ha ha; well . . . . Look what I've done to myself, uh I'm not here right now better talk to me more tomorrow . . . . no, no, better make it tomorrow afternoon."

Brian stuttered, "Do . . . do you always do this after you win a battle?"

"Win? Oh no Brian, no one ever wins. If you return with everyone you left with, you break even. But win? Oh no, son." His eyes began to close and he mumbled himself to sleep. "Thoughtfulness is the soil from which wisdom may grrrow . . . Brrri . . ."

"It doesn't look like he'll have too much more to say tonight," Brian said aloud. He walked toward the crackling fireplace. He lay down and curled up in a tuft of warm moss and drifted to sleep.

At dawn, Brian was awakened by the grunts and groans of the Thorks, who were trying to get the dampness out of their heads. Brian sat up and saw Slizard hobbling over to him while trying to get a kink out of his neck.

"Uh, morning Brian," he said, clearing his throat and rubbing his eyes. "Well, what did you find out about our guest?"

"I tried to tell you last night but . . ."

"I know," interrupted Slizard. "Go on."

"Well, it turns out she's King Bara's daughter Cassie."

"Cassie Bara?!" exclaimed Slizard. His words set all the ears in the room to ringing, in more ways than one.

"Yeah, that's her. You see, she and I made this deal that if I went back as her prisoner, she would free Tommy and me before sacrifice."

"Are you kidding? It doesn't sound like much of a deal to me."

"But it's the only way I can get Tommy out! She won't do it any other way and she gave me her word!"

"You take the word of a Trediarian! She has evil in her eyes. I saw it."

"Sliz, I . . ."

Slizard interrupted. "I insist that if you must be so foolhardy you take Ebil for good luck."

"Ebil?" questioned Brian.

"Yes," said Slizard, grinning. "Ebil J. Yabut himself! We need the luck around here, but nothing like you're going to need."

"No, I really shouldn't," said Brian, trying to get out of it.

"I insist," said Slizard.

"Thanks," Brian said, pretending to be appreciative.

"Ebil!" screamed Slizard. Ebil appeared from behind his shoulder.

"At your service, Sire."

Slizard turned to Ebil. "You shall accompany Brian to the castle."

"Oh no!" said Ebil, backing up and raising his hands in defense. "The Raven can't fly through infinity's eye, so we will die!"

"Is he serious?" said Brian

"I'm afraid so," said Slizard, shaking this gray head. "Well then, you'd better get started before sacrifice."

Brian nodded and walked toward Cassie's cell. He thought about what Slizard and Ebil had said as he made his way through the darkened halls. He turned the rusty key in the big wooden door and pulled it open.

"Well, it's about time!" she said, standing with her hands on her hips.

"What do you mean?" Brian asked.

"You said you'd be right back! And I've been waiting here all night!"

"Uh, sorry," he said, not knowing what else to say.

"Well?" She snapped.

"It's okay with Slizard, but we have to take a crazy man with us."

"Good! We can use the luck." With that she marched out of her cell ahead of him.

The way she took command all the time irritated Brian. He let her walk ahead of him and after a while she became bewildered and lost in the tunnel. Finally, as he had hoped, she turned to him for assistance.

"How do we get out of this stinky hole?" she asked.

Brian smiled and took his place in front. "Follow me," he said, sensing he had taught her a lesson, at least for now.

They found Slizard, Razz and Ebil in the main room with a number of others. "Sorry to see ya go, kid," said Razz. "You can still change your mind you know."

"No thanks," replied Brian.

"Well, I want ya to have this," he said, handing Brian a handsome red cloak.

"Thanks," smiled Brian, accepting it willingly. "It's really soft," he said, as he tried it on. "Hey! There's a band around the arm."

"Consideration," Slizard responded. "It's a wonderful gesture, you risking your life for your brother. Now, take your sword and Ebil and be on your way."

Meanwhile, Razz pulled a sash from his robe and tied it around the girl's head covering her eyes. Brian and Ebil led her up the tunnel to the forest above.

Suddenly they were alone in the quiet forest. The sun shone off Brian's saber and the wind glided through Cassie's hair.

They began weaving through a maze of trees and leafy bushes. Cassie held Brian's hand as he led the way.

Her foot caught in a vine and she flopped to the ground. "Will you watch where I'm going!" she yelled.

"Don't get your feathers ruffled, Black Witch!" said Ebil as he helped Cassie off the ground.

Cassie stammered, "Black Witch! Where did you hear that?"

"A little bird told me."

Cassie turned her head to where she thought Brian was standing. "Did you tell him, Brian?"

"I'm not the bird he's talking about; no telling how or what he knows."

"Well I've gone far enough and I'm taking this thing off." She pulled the sash from her head and marched ahead to the edge of the forest.

Brian and Ebil caught up with her as they entered the tall grasses and began walking down into the valley. Cassie turned to Brian as he parted the tall blades of grass.

"You're pretty tall to be a Thork," she said.

"That's 'cause I'm not," Brian replied.

"If you're not, then where did you come from?"

"A small hole in a pond . . . somewhere . . ."

"Aw, you don't know where you're from, do you?"

"No, I know where I'm from. I just don't know where I am."

Ebil spoke up. "Are you in reality or in a dream? I can always tell if I'm in reality because the rules are much stiffer than in dreams, yes, much stiffer."

"When I'm in a dream, I'm asleep!" said Brian.

"Are you asleep now?"

"No," said Brian.

"Well then," Ebil grinned, "We all know where you are; you're in reality."

"Thanks a lot."

He looked across the sky for the reddish orange clouds. A few splotches could be seen here and there but none looked too threatening. "Why do you worship those clouds?" he asked.

"Because they protect us from all evils," said Cassie.

"But the clouds are evil!"

"Only to those who don't believe; you see, those who don't believe in Nimbus as a cloud god have meaningless lives and must perish so they don't sway the minds of us who are the true believers."

"That's pretty dumb!" Brian remarked.

Cassie became angry. "It's not dumb. It is my creed. If we do something wrong, we give sacrifice to Nimbus and then we're even up again."

"Cassie," said Brian, pausing to arrange his thoughts. "It's not important to give sacrifice or believe in a cloud; what is important is believing in yourself, knowing who you are inside . . . a good person, I hope. If you do something wrong and truly regret your actions, that's what it's all about. You decide what kind of person you want to be. That is your target. That is what you try to hit. You may miss once in awhile but that does not mean you stop aiming. Giving sacrifices doesn't change who you are."

Cassie became confused. "If I don't believe in Nimbus I'll die; because he won't protect me!"

"He never did, witch," Ebil said.

Cassie pushed Ebil away. "My father warned me about non-believers and their evil swaying ways."

"As a guide," said Brian. "Any belief system that has you killing anyone who thinks differently than you . . . um . . . I would stay away from."

Ebil licked his knobby finger and held it up as if to check the direction of the wind and said, "Everyone with different beliefs.

Everyone thinks they are right but everyone can't be right, can they? The truth lies within the similarities not the differences. It is where they intersect that you will find the truth."

They had crossed the valley and were starting up the long slithering path that led through jagged rocks toward the castle.

Cassie took the sword from Brian and had him and Ebil walk in front of her so they would look like her captives.

The castle looked ghastly, with towering, twisted walls that appeared to grow right up out of the mountain. Brian cringed; there was something lifeless and horrible about it he didn't like. It was a kind of ghastly feeling, an ugliness. To make matters worse, Ebil began to chant, to remove his mind from the unpleasant experience.

"I'm going on an endless dream, where anything can be done and anything can be seen. Where my mind is free to roam and leave my body in bed at home. If I return I do not care because even now . . . I drift far, far away from there. I will search the endless pathways of my mind and drift in the peace I will find. Reality and dreams, here's where they differ, in reality, the rules are stiffer."

Cassie led them up the winding path until they stood directly in front of the castle looking up at the dark monstrosity.

Two giant prehistoric animals blocked two towering spiked doors. The beasts were held by large iron chains around their necks. Their tongues lashed out and their mindless cold eyes peered at them, straining on their chains, clawing and frothing at the mouth. They looked like mythical Dragons but had no wings and didn't spit fire.

"Are those gargons?" asked Brian.

"Yes," Cassie answered, appearing surprised by the question.

Cassie waved her sword to a guard on the castle wall and the chains holding the gargons snapped taut. Clanking chains pulled the gargons away from the huge doors. The two grotesque monsters were pulled into two caves, one on each side of the doors. Cassie nudged Brian forward with the tip of the sword.

"Ouch! Watch it, will ya!" said Brian. "It hurts you know!"

"They don't call her witch for nothing," said Ebil.

"Shut up and walk," Cassie ordered.

An ancient creaking noise whined as the mighty doors began to open. A breath of stale air rushed out as if escaping. "Inside," ordered Cassie. They stepped through the doors and into the castle.

Chapter Four

Exodus

The doors of the tomb-like castle closed behind the trio, trapping them hopelessly inside. Engulfed by darkness, Brian strained to see. "Where are we?" he asked, his words lingering in the moist stale air. Cassie remained silent.

His heard footsteps growing louder and louder. Something was coming out of the darkness; it was something sinister. He shuddered to think what might happen to him if Cassie had tricked them. "Slizard said she had evil in her eyes," he thought. "I hope I'm not wrong about her."

Brian jerked forward as the tip of a needle-sharp blade pricked his back. "This way," echoed a voice. "Cassie, your father wants to see you immediately!" said another voice. Brian heard Cassie sigh as she walked briskly off.

"Don't forget!" Brian yelled to her.

Blinded in the darkness, Brian and Ebil were guided up a long circular stairway by a pair of Black Knights. They came to a door made of thick iron bars. A knight jiggled a set of rusty keys, opened the door, and shoved them inside.

"I wonder how many creatures have spent their final hours here?" said Ebil. The door slammed behind them and the keys clanked as the knights locked the door, then quietly walked away.

The cell was small and round with piles of hay spread in clumps across the floor. The walls were square stone blocks with moss eaten cracks. The only window was threaded with steel bars. Warm sunlight streamed in, casting lined shadows.

Brian saw something move in the corner. "Brian?" said a voice.

"Tommy?" he answered. The shadow moved. It was his Tommy! "You're all right! Aren't you?"

"Yes," Tommy exclaimed, jumping to his feet.

Brian gave him a huge hug. "How did we ever get into this mess, Tom?"

"How did you find me?" Tommy smiled.

Brian tried to explain. "Well, I kept hearing this voice when the wind blew. And uh . . . I don't know!"

Tommy cut in, "I bet Mom is worried about us."

"Yeah," Brian answered. "She should be!" He walked over and looked out the window. They were in a tower that stretched straight up into the sky. The castle had many other towers but only one was taller than theirs. A narrow stairway stretched across the sky connecting their tower with the tallest one. It had ancient writing on the side and was bowl shaped at the top. "Looks like we're connected to some kind of altar," he said.

The skyline was cut by a massive stone mountain. On the ledge outside the window were man-sized squatting stone gargoyles. They looked like evil demons, just waiting for the chance to pounce. "Hideous!" he thought to himself.

Ebil slid down the wall into a pile of hay. "Say! What's the buzz, bumble bee?" he said to Tommy while making a demented, snarling face.

"Who's he, Brian?" Tommy asked backing away.

"Oh, I'm sorry. Don't mind him. He's nuts."

"Are you sure?"

"I'm sure," interrupted Ebil, "but is a madman sure of anything if he's sure he's mad?"

Tommy wrinkled his forehead. "You're right Brian, he's weird!"

"At first they said he was very dangerous, but now I don't think so," Brian said, sitting down in the hay.

"Are you sure?" said Tommy, standing a safe distance.

"Yeah, I'm pretty sure. He saved my life."

"How?" Tommy asked.

Brian began to explain everything that had happened to him, and then Tommy told of his own strange happenings.

After listening to Brian and Tommy talk, Ebil said, "Black birds and bumble bees have changed their domain? It must be a strain!"

Tommy looked at Brian, as if to say, "This guy's crazy!"

"You'll get used to him," said Brian.

"Have you?" Tommy asked.

"Well . . . no," Brian admitted.

"Are you sure this girl is going to come back to free us?"

"I think so," Brian muttered.

Tommy became upset. "You think so! Where is she? If she doesn't come, how will we get out of here?"

Ebil sat in the corner making strange shapes with strands of hay.

"Relax!" Brian assured him. "If she double crossed me I'll get us out of here . . . there has to be a way." Brian walked to the window, looking for an answer. He grasped the sun-warmed bars and looked at the gargoyles hunched over the ledge. He could see their age in the cracks that wound around them like vines. One of them had apparently fallen off the ledge because only half of its decaying trunk remained. The gargoyle nearest the window had a crack that ran through its stone mouth, which made it appear to be grinning. "I wonder what he's smiling about?" Brian thought.

Night began to fall and Cassie had not yet come to free them.

"When is she supposed to come?" Tommy asked.

"After dinner," Ebil replied. "She's shiny red evil, I could feel it! But then . . . I have been wrong before," he said, while digging his finger in his ear.

"I think she'll be here!" Brian stammered.

"Shhhh, someone's coming!" Ebil gurgled. "It's probably meal time for Nimbus."

A Black Knight arrived at the door. "Don't sacrifice us," Tommy burst. "Use a cow or lamb or something."

The knight slid a tray of steaming food under the door, and they gave a sigh of relief.

"We eat the food today, and we are the food tomorrow," Ebil laughed.

Brian stared at the wall. "I wish the wind would whisper a way for us to get out of here."

"I'm sure this castle is full of weary spirits. Maybe one of them will help us," Ebil suggested.

"We'll have a better chance with spirits than with that dumb girl," Tommy said sarcastically.

Brian thought for a moment, and then said, "Yeah, but she seemed so sincere."

Ebil cackled, "A pretty face, a deceptive image. Treds are very cunning and ruthless."

"I'm not ready to die!" Tommy whined, tears escaping from his eyes.

"Yes, yes, she was pretty as a song, but it was a funeral dirge," Ebil continued.

"Will you shut up!" Brian yelled.

"Brian," whispered a soft voice. He turned and saw Cassie kneeling at the steel door. She handed him a massive rope through the iron bars. "You'll need this to escape."

Brian smiled. "I knew you'd come."

"Careful, it's a trick!" said Ebil.

Cassie fumbled to find the right key but the big ring slipped from her fingers, clanking to the ground.

They listened for a moment. "Someone's coming!" she said, "Hide the rope!"

Brian quickly buried it under a pile of hay.

"I'll be back," she said. She turned to leave but bumped into a knight blocking her path.

He snatched her into the air with one arm as she thrashed about. "What's this?" he said, prying the keys from her clenched fist. "You stole my keys! Your father must know of this grave error in judgment."

"No," Cassie cried. "He'll kill me!"

"You must accept your punishment!" growled the guard as he carried her kicking body down the stairs.

"Cassie," Brian called out, but she was already gone.

Cassie was taken to an elegant room where her ogre-like father sat alone at his lavish table. He ate chunks of snake meat with his fingers and gulped from a big goblet. The knight crashed through the large double doors clutching Cassie by the arm.

"What is it?" the king demanded, a piece of snakeskin dangling from his open mouth.

"I followed her like you said, and caught her trying to free the Thorks from the tower dungeon."

"Very well!" bellowed the King. "Now be gone!" The knight turned sharply and walked toward the doors, Cassie following.

"No! You, my dark daughter shall remain!" He choked on some meat, cleared his throat then recklessly drank wine from the goblet.

Cassie moved toward the table and stood in front of her father.

"On your knees, witch!" he screamed. She fell to her knees sobbing. "Your mother died so you could be born and now I suppose you plan to kill me too with your Thork friends!"

"No Father!" she pleaded. "I captured them to please you!"

"And I suppose you tried to free them to please me?" he said, taking a large bite of meat. "No . . . no daughter, I don't trust you. You're no better than those scruds you tried to free!"

"Daddy, I only wanted you to love me."

"Cassie," he said, pointing down at her with a greasy finger. "You don't know how to love. You are a dark witch! As Leether the nimbian priest said, you will someday bring great carnage upon this place. You will

Chapter Four

be placed on the altar tomorrow with the Thorks for sacrifice. Innocent or guilty, Nimbus will decide your punishment."

"No!" she cried. "You're insane! I haven't done anything to harm you. You're losing your mind, Father."

"I don't want to hear any more!" he screeched. "Nimbus will pass judgment."

"Take this traitor to the tower dungeon!"

The doors opened and knights and servants entered the room to fulfill his requests. Cassie, screaming and kicking, was dragged from the room. "More snake!" she heard him yell as she was pulled roughly down the hall.

"Well, look who's here," said Ebil, relaxing in the corner with a piece of hay sticking in his mouth. The door squeaked open and the knight threw Cassie in. She fell hard face down.

Tommy looked irritated. "Now how are we going to get out?"

When the knight left Brian knelt by Cassie. "Are you okay?" he asked tenderly. She lifted her bowed head and looked into Brian's eyes. Her face was contorted and tears dripped off her warm damp skin.

"Now Nimbus is going to eat me too!" she cried.

Ebil casually took the hay from his mouth. "I thought Nimbus didn't eat those who truly believe."

"Shut up!" she bellowed in frustration.

"Cassie, look," said Brian, "You've lived here all your life. You must know some trick to get us out of here."

"I can't remember anyone ever escaping,"

"But they've never had us as captives before," he said, trying to give her a little confidence.

"Just leave me alone for a while, will you?"

Brian sighed, then walked to his brother and sat down.

Tommy whispered, "She's a real snot isn't she, Brian?"

"Yup," he said, shaking his head.

Tommy grinned. "But you kind of like her, don't you?"

"Are you kidding?" Brian said.

The hours passed and the sun began to set behind the mountains.

Cassie stood up, wiped her swollen eyes, and then walked over to the barred window. Brian and Tommy watched as Ebil snored in the corner. She stood motionless, gazing out and thinking.

"What is it?" Brian asked.

She sniffed. "We'll be sacrificed at morning light, when the first stream of light passes over the horizon."

"How will they do it?"

"They'll take us across that stairway to the altar, tie us down and light four urns. The oil from the urns will give off blue smoke and the smoke will draw Nimbus. When he approaches a big gong will sound and everyone will watch and cheer as we're devoured by him."

"Wonderful!" said Brian, making a face.

"This is what I get for trying to save you!" she shouted. "I get put on the altar by my own father!"

Brian was enraged. "But that was our deal! Now sit down and be quiet! Complaining isn't going to get us out of here. We're gonna have to work together, and that's the way it has to be." Cassie, startled by the outburst, sat down in the hay.

"We could tie the rope to the door and all pull on it together," Tommy suggested.

"I'll try anything, but I'll never give up." Brian said, glancing at Cassie out of the corner of his eye. Ebil woke from his slumber and groggily watched as Brian tied the thick rope to the door. He made knot upon knot, until he felt it wouldn't come undone.

"Let's give it a yank," said Brian.

Cassie slowly crawled to her feet. Ebil spoke to Cassie while rotating his head like a cocker spaniel. "Come witch, don't be beaten, show some effort or you'll be eaten." Then Ebil laughed hysterically.

They all pulled together on the rope, but the door stood like a rock. "We don't have the strength to pull it out," said Brian, perspiration dripping from his face.

"We'll tie Cassie to the other end of the rope and throw her out the window," suggested Ebil. "That'll jerk the door."

"If we throw something heavy out that window, tied to the other end of the rope, it would really pull on that door," said Brian.

"Cassie's heavy," said Ebil with his toothy grin.

Cassie frowned. "First, there's nothing heavy in here, and second, how would we fit it through the bars on the window?"

"I don't know," Brian answered.

Ebil made a buzzing fly noise then gurgled, "The answer lies within the cracks of the ledge, vulture."

Brian ran to the window. "The gargoyle on the ledge is ready to fall! If I could lasso it, maybe we could pull it off the ledge. When it falls and the rope runs out it'll really yank on that door."

Cassie spoke up: "I hope that gargoyle is cracked all the way through. It might be . . . they're always falling off the ledges . . . It's a good idea, Brian."

"Ebil thought of it," he answered.

"Think we're strong enough to pull it off the ledge?" Tommy asked.

"That all depends on the gargoyle," said Brian.

With one end of the rope secured to the cell door, Brian began making a lasso with the other.

Tommy smiled. "It'll be just like roping pigs, won't it Brian? Brian's real good at that."

"What's a pig?" Cassie asked?

"Why, your father is, dear," Ebil interrupted.

Tommy and Brian laughed. "How do you know what a pig is?" Tommy asked.

"I am mad, bumble. I can see things no one else can, I can, I can and even if I can't, well, I still can. I can see even with my eyes closed, but can I see with them open? Well . . . that's another matter; another matter indeed," Ebil chuckled to himself.

"I think I know what you mean," said Tommy.

"You're in worse shape than he is," Cassie said sarcastically.

"Okay," said Brian, standing up and testing the knots. He stretched his arm and shoulder through the bars as far as he could and lightly tossed the lasso toward the gargoyle. The rope drifted over the top, missing.

Cassie looked at Brian. "If we can just get the door open I think I can get us out of here."

Brian nodded. Cassie peered out the window. "I hope the rope doesn't snap when the gargoyle falls and the rope runs out."

Brian concentrated and tried again and this time the rope looped around the grotesque frozen beast. Brian pulled hard to set the knot. The gargoyle began to crumble from the ledge.

"It's coming down already!" screamed Brian.

"Move!" Cassie yelled.

The gargoyle tumbled free and the rope was quickly sucked from the window.

Brian shoved Cassie and Tommy out of the way as Ebil remained relaxed in the corner.

With a large explosion the door flew out of the wall, sailed across the cell and slammed into the barred window.

"Come!" said Cassie, running through the opening as splinters rained down. Brian stumbled off, followed by Ebil and Tommy. Cassie looked over her shoulder to see that they were coming. "Follow me and I'll get us out of here," she said nervously.

Up the ancient stairs they ran, hearts pounding. It was very dark and the thought of something unknown leaping out of the darkness made Brian leery.

"Brian?" Are you there?" said Tommy.

"I'm right in front of you, Tom."

"And I'm right behind you," cackled Ebil.

Cassie led them through an oval doorway high in the tower. The stairway led straight through the air connecting their tower with the top of the altar.

"I'm not going across there!" Tommy announced.

"Just don't look down," Cassie assured, "It's our best way out."

The gargoyle dangled from the window rocking to and fro. Tommy looked down. Tiny people moved back and forth on the ground below. The four ran across the open stairway.

They quickly arrived at the top of the altar. In the center was a basin with ropes to tie down victims. Four black urns filled with blue oil sat around the edge and four crackling torches stood between them. Darkness had begun to fall on the castle as the sun fell away beyond the mountaintops.

"Listen to me," said Cassie, "and maybe I can get us out of this mess. Light the urns and dump them over the side; the smoke draws Nimbus."

"Like catnip?" said Brian.

"It'll cause confusion and give us time. Save the last one though; we may need it later on."

They quickly did as she asked. Tommy lit an urn and poured the flaming blue oil over the edge. It fell a long time. The oil slapped against the ground, flames squirting in all directions. Huge rolling balls of blue-gray smoke began crawling up the side of the tower.

"Get that last urn, grab some rope and come on!" she yelled. Ebil struggled to wind the large rope around his shoulders.

"Okay, which way do we go?" Brian asked.

"First we've got to get Snookems," she said.

"Snookems?"

"Yeah, my animal. I can't leave without my pet."

"Forget your animal!" Brian yelled.

"Please! It's on the way and it won't hurt anything."

Ebil grimaced. "Only the length of our lives."

Chapter Four

"If my pet doesn't go, neither do I!" she said, glaring at Brian.

"Fine with me," said Ebil. "Don't come with us."

"Yeah," Tommy agreed.

Brian moaned. He could hear noises from below growing louder. "Cassie, you'll be killed if you stay!"

"Don't argue with her," Ebil interrupted.

"But she knows the way out of here!" Brian pleaded. Red clouds could be seen drifting over the mountains. "It's on the way."

Cassie grinned. "Follow me. It won't take long, you'll see." She ran down a corridor in the altar basin, followed closely by Brian, Tommy and Ebil.

They ran for several minutes through a maze of tower stairs, corridors and entranceways. They passed several people who did not appear to notice them in the confusion.

Loud gongs began sounding in rapid succession.

Cassie smiled. "Nimbus must be over the castle."

They dashed up a circular stairway with marble walls on both sides. Clanging armor could now be heard behind them around every turn. With knights hot on their heels, they reached the top of the stairs.

"Brian, get ready with the urn," Cassie said, pulling a torch from the wall.

A swarm of knights rounded the corner from out of the shadows.

Brian raised the urn. "Wait!" Cassie said. "Not yet!" Every second brought them closer. They growled and grunted like a pack of dogs as they charged up the steps. Their mouths were wide and angry; a death wish gleamed in their eyes.

"Now!" she yelled. Brian threw the shiny urn down the stairs. It shattered into a million pieces, sounding like a wind chime in a whirlwind. Blue oil coated the steps from wall to wall, but did not slow the approaching executioners.

Cassie cocked back and whistled the torch down the stairs at their angry faces. An instantaneous wall of fire rose in front of them. Brian could see dark blurry shapes struggling and falling into the hot engulfing flames. Blue-gray smoke bellowed up the stairway in thick spinning balls.

They ran up the stairs onto a large balcony. It had a full-length window in the back and overlooked the throne room in the front. Thirty-foot fur curtains hung on both sides of the balcony down to the empty throne room.

"Can you get us out of here?" Brian asked.

"I used to play here, so no problem," Cassie said.

The window suddenly shattered behind them and a red cloud began oozing in.

"Oh no!" said Cassie, clasping her hand to her face. She ran to the edge of the balcony, hung out over the railing and grabbed onto the curtains. She slid down the curtains and dropped to the hard marble floor of the throne room. The rest of them, choking on smoke, wasted no time following.

Tommy let go of the curtain and landed on his feet next to Cassie. "Okay, where's your dumb pet!"

"This way," she said, leading them to her father's throne. She walked around to the back of the plush throne and pushed aside fur curtains.

Behind the curtains was an elegant room. They entered apprehensively. The curtains dropped in place and muffled the screams from the clouds' attack of the castle.

The room was small for royalty, with golden candlesticks, a mirror, soft rug and canopied bed. There was a fat cat-like creature with a forked tail and eagle like tallons curled up on a pillow.

Chapter Four

Tommy glanced around. "Is this the King's room?"

"It's mine," Cassie answered. "Snookie?" she called out, getting nothing but a cranky glance from the animal. Cassie went over to where it lay. "Come Snooks, we've . . ."

"Got to leave now," Brian interrupted.

The overweight cat rolled on this back and stretched. "Raoowoo."

Cassie reached down to pick up the cat while Ebil glared at it. "Here Kitty," he growled, revealing his crooked teeth. The skittish animal looked at Ebil and leaped from the bed away from Cassie's grasp.

"Snookie!!"

Brian, meanwhile, examined a sword and spear decoration that hung on the wall.

"Hey! This is like the sword Slizard gave me." He lifted the thick saber from the wall, and when he did the spear fell to the ground. "We can use this too," Brian said, leaning the spear against the wall behind him.

Cassie felt a familiar hand on her shoulder. She turned to see her father standing behind her.

He grabbed a handful of her hair and pulled her head toward him. "One more move from you and she dies," he said, pointing the tip of his sword at the group. "You witch! You black-hearted, hell-born witch!" he shouted. "You destroy everything!"

"No, Daddy!

He pulled her by the hair, tilting her head back to expose her bare neck. He raised his sword.

"Daughter, the Nimbian priest says I must finish you!"

"Dad, no! You're insane! Can't you see what you're doing?"

Ebil slipped his hand around his back and grabbed the spear that leaned against the wall. The King's hand trembled for a moment, as he wrestled with his conscience.

Ebil lurched forward throwing the spear inches over Cassie's arched body into the armored chest of her father. "Ugh!"

King Bara stumbled back, clutching the spear, and fell to the floor. He struggled to sit up. The King rasped as he breathed and winced with pain as he spoke. "You'll all pay for this! No, you won't get away! I'll get you! It may not be today or tomorrow, but I'll make you wish you died on the altar today."

Ebil rolled his eyes. "Aw, shut up!"

"Let's get!" said Brian. Ebil walked to the King and disrespectfully pushed him down with his foot. The King stared at him, not knowing what to expect.

Ebil planted one foot on the King's chest and jerked the spear out. Ebil grinned. "We might need this spear later. Shouldn't waste it."

"I'll send the Nimbus priest after you!" gurgled the King, propping himself back up.

"Why?" Cassie asked, tears beginning to form at the corners of her eyes.

Ebil turned around with the spear and crackled, "Well, what if we just disappear, just dis right appear?"

"That's what you'll have to do or the priest will find you. I wish you great pain as he gives your bodies to Nimbus!"

Tommy shivered.

Cassie turned away, her eyes damp. "Follow me to the wall . . ." she mumbled.

"Are you okay?" Brian asked, putting reassuring arm on her shoulder.

"Come on," she said, "we've got to get going."

They followed Cassie as she ran through a door to the walkway along the castle wall. The cloud was rising off the castle and screaming people were running everywhere.

"A red curtain of death," Ebil mumbled. It was a mass of confusion, but that's the way they wanted it.

Brian took the rope off Ebil's shoulder, tied the end around a notch in the wall, then dropped the rest over the edge.

"I don't know if I can make it!" said Tommy.

"Sure you can," answered Cassie. "We used to do this for fun. Now just do as I do." She slid over the wall with ease and began crawling down.

Ebil looked over the edge at the long descent. "We mustn't build walls, for someday we may be required to climb them."

"Hurry up!" said Brian. He lifted Tommy over the edge and he frantically grabbed the rope.

"Now don't be afraid; just concentrate on what you're doing," Brian assured his brother. "Here they come!" he said, as he saw a knight running along the wall toward them. "Well, I'm gone," he said, slipping over the edge.

Ebil readied his spear. He sent it sailing through the air, well over the knight's head. "Missed," he grumbled, jumping over the side and snagging the rope on the way down.

Tommy and Cassie jumped to the ground. Brian looked up while continuing to climb down and saw the knight staring down at him. Ebil, realizing the knight was about to cut the rope, began sliding down at an almost falling pace. Then the end of the rope came floating over the wall. The tension on the rope was suddenly gone, and they fell the last 16 feet. They landed hard and rolled, shaken but unhurt.

The remaining rope rained down on them like a spaghetti shower.

"I forgot Snookems!" Cassie cried.

"How fortunate," Ebil yelped. Cassie frowned. Ebil coiled up the rope as they scrambled under the trees at the base of the mountain.

They sat in the shadows, to plot their next move as the wind screamed through the rocks and branches. Tommy glanced at Brian.

"Brian, I want to go home!"

"We've got to get through that membrane first," Brian sighed.

The wind howled through the trees saying, "Follow me, follow me, for the key, follow me."

"It's that voice again!" Brian gasped.

"What did it say?" Tommy asked.

"Follow me for the key! Which way is the wind blowing?"

Ebil licked his thumb and held it up. "Straight up the mountain."

"Good!" said Brian. "The key to opening the membrane could be up this mountain somewhere."

"I'm not going!" Cassie said.

"I'm sorry," said Brian, "but we're all you got. You don't have anywhere else to go."

She dropped her head, and then followed them through the trees.

Chapter Five

The Dangling

Cassie had known it would happen some day. She had dreaded it, dreamed about it, feared it and now it was happening. She was leaving the castle, never to return.

Brian lifted her between the jagged crevices as they began making their way up the rocky slope.

The deadly cloud hung above the castle and began to rumble. Lightning spurted from its mass, flashing light into the now darkened sky.

"It's going to rain," muttered Cassie.

"Obviously," remarked Ebil.

"Why are we doing this?" Cassie asked.

"Huh?" said Brian puzzled.

"Why are we climbing this stupid mountain?" she burst as she strained to pull herself up on a rock. "Because the wind told you to? I don't conceive this!"

"You've got a point," said Ebil, raising his crooked index finger. "But if you comb your hair right and wear a helmet, maybe nobody will notice."

She thought for a moment, and then frowned. "Brian, do you know what's on the other side? Do you know why no one dares to venture over this mountain?!"

"Gargons?" asked Brian.

"Yes!" she said. "Huge drooling, stomping gargons! Not to mention a full assortment of other evil beasts."

Tommy turned to Ebil for confirmation. "Are there really gargons over there Ebil?"

"Yesss," he hissed like a snake, glaring into Tommy's young eyes. "They come at you in a mindless, senseless daze, with dull lifeless eyes. They stare, stare right into your soul, cold and damp they are . . . like death itself." Tommy's mouth dropped open.

Ebil gurgled, pointing down at the castle. "Look! A row of torches follows us up the mountain."

"It's the Nimbus priest, Leether," Cassie said solemnly. "My father has sent him to see justice is done for Nimbus."

"Justice?" said Tommy, wrinkling his forehead.

Cassie clarified. "To see that the cloud eats us. They can't return to the castle until they have our bodies alive or . . . otherwise."

"Goodbye!" said Tommy, scrambling up between the rocks.

"Wait up!" Brian yelled.

Chapter Five

Tommy climbed a few more feet then yelled, "Hey, there's a path up here!"

Indeed there was a path; an ancient one that looked like it hadn't been used for decades. It dipped in and out of the jagged rocks, going up and around the outside of the nearly vertical mountain.

It was dark and the footing was unstable. Cassie led them up the uneven path for an hour or so as thunder rumbled in the heavens.

"This rain could make it rough," Brian said.

"And wet," said Ebil.

"We could probably make it in the rain, but it's going to get awfully slippery," Brian muttered, kicking up the soil.

"Don't take unnecessary chances," Ebil cackled "Save yourself for the necessary ones."

"Over here!" Cassie said, looking under an overhanging slab along the path. "This may do." The slab was angled down about three feet off the ground and there was plenty of room to hide underneath it.

Lightning crackled across the black night sky. The air seemed to shiver as thunder boomed, disrupting the dark stillness.

"Quick! Before we get drenched," said Cassie, crawling under the rock.

"Do you think they'll come looking for us?" Brian asked.

"Not in the rain because they could get washed right off the path."

"But you never know," Ebil muttered.

"You never know," Cassie agreed.

They all fit snugly under the slab. It was dark and moist, but free of slimy crawly things and it felt safe. Then it rained hard as it always did after the cloud had its fill . . .

Cassie lay on her side, lost in thought, watching the rain sliding down the jagged rocks. She thought about what might lie over the mountain, and the Nimbus priest and the Black Knights. "Will they track us forever? And what if we're caught?" She assumed her father was alive and would stay that way. He was a survivor. "The mean die hard," she thought.

Tommy lay on his back staring into the blackness. He thought about home and wondered where it was. He thought about his mother and what she must be thinking.

Brian and Ebil were sound asleep. Brian's arm twitched now and then and Ebil spoke aloud in words without connection, in mysterious voices that didn't sound like his own.

The night passed quietly and morning came. The sun peeked slowly over the mountain. Streams of light slid under the overlaying rock waking Ebil.

"Rise and fall," Ebil grinned, cocking his head slightly to the right.

Cassie groaned, feeling the dampness that had settled into her bones.

They crawled out from under the rock. Brian sucked in the cool morning air. Ebil laid the flat edge of the sword across one shoulder and the wound rope around the other.

Tommy looked back down the path. "How far behind us do you think those knights are, Brian?"

Ebil answered for Brian: "Not close enough to smell you, yet not so far as not to know where you have been!"

Chapter Five

"Exactly," said Brian. Tommy giggled at Ebil and fell in line behind him as they started up the path.

The path was narrow and uneven. At times the mountain was on one side and the other side was open air. The mountain was full of strange rock formations carved by wind and water. Brush grew out of the cracks. Towers of rock stretched straight up in the air from far below. These rock towers stood tall, unyielding to the natural forces that made them.

All morning and most of the afternoon they walked up the long winding path.

"Do you think Mom and Grandma miss us back home?" Tommy asked.

"They think we're dead!" Brian replied.

"Maybe you are," Ebil cackled.

"No!" Tommy yelled, "No! We're not!"

"Shhh." The knights may hear us, Brian cautioned."

"At least you have a home to go back to," said Cassie. "I have nothing."

"I know something about nothing," Ebil gurgled. He moved his head and hands rhythmically as he spoke. "In the beginning there was nothing . . . But after a time something began to appear, and with this something came responsibility, and with this responsibility came problems. With these problems came thoughts and with these thoughts came solutions. With these solutions came accomplishment and with this accomplishment came confidence. And within this confidence is the tranquility of spirit." It was quiet for a moment as they took in what Ebil said.

Tommy tapped Cassie on the shoulder. "We've got an extra room on the farm." Brian smiled to himself.

"What's a farm?" she asked.

"Well," Tommy began, "it's a place where you grow plants and animals."

Cassie frowned. "Animals and plants grow all by themselves."

Brian turned around to explain. "No, they need . . ." Just then his foot slipped on a small rock and he slid off the crumbling path and into the vastness of open space. He clawed frantically at loose dirt on the edge of the path as it gave way.

"Brian!" Cassie yelled, "Hold on!" Tommy reached for his hand but it was too late.

"Oh my God!" Brian yelled as he disappeared over the edge. All that remained was a horrible deadly silence. Tommy could not believe it. His brother would always be immortal, indestructible, yet he was gone.

"Oh my . . ." said Ebil, calmly scratching his chin.

Cassie dropped to her knees and dared to peer over the edge. "Oh, thank you! Thank you!" she said. Brian lay sprawled on top of a towering rock 20 feet below.

"Are you okay?" Tommy yelled down.

"I'm alive!" Brian screamed.

"Anything broken?" Cassie asked.

"I hurt everywhere, but I think everything still works." He got up slowly, groaning as he moved. He was so close to them, yet separated by 20 feet of open air.

"Brian!" yelled Tommy. "We'll get ya. Ebil's still got the rope."

Brian looked over the edge of the rock tower, knowing that far, far beneath the mist was the ground. He stepped back and wiped the nervous perspiration from his face.

Chapter Five

The sun was beginning to set as Ebil looped the rope around a fallen rock slab big enough to walk behind. Tommy tied dozens of knots while Cassie knelt on the edge silently watching.

"I hope you're not afraid of heights, Raven," said Ebil, grinning as he heaved the rope over the edge. It thumped hard on the rock below. Brian pulled the rope taunt, testing its stability.

"The Raven can't fly!" whined Ebil. Brian looked up.

"Anything else, Ebil?"

"Don't glance under, don't decline."

"Just pretend you're climbing the barn," said Tommy. As Brian pulled himself up, his weight carried him off the towering rock out into the open air and nothingness. Brian glanced down, knowing the rock was no longer there to catch him.

"Don't glance under!" barked Ebil.

Straining with each pull, hand over hand Brian came closer and closer to them . . .

"Voices . . . I hear strange voices," Cassie whispered, turning her head quickly. Tommy gave her a blank look.

Cassie put a comforting hand on Tommy's shoulder. "Climb up into the rocks and hide," she said. "Ebil, cover the rope!"

She boosted Tommy up between the jagged rocks then followed him.

Brian remained suspended in the air, swinging to and fro with the cool mountain breezes.

On came the grave voices conversing soberly. "Come on Pug or we're leaving you behind!"

Ebil hurriedly covered the rope stretched across the path with loose dirt and brushed off their tracks. He tucked himself and the sword behind the rock slab and put a small tuft of brush in front of him.

Cassie peeked over the edge of the jagged rock. "The Nimbus priest," she said quietly. "Leether . . . the Father of Death and Darkness."

She could see Leether strutting out ahead of the knights, the wind blowing through his blood-red cape. He carried a torch and a twisted black staff with a golden knob on top. He looked too tall to be one of the Treds. Tommy saw a bitterness that showed in the lines of his weathered face. Behind him were the Black Knights with swords and flickering torches that lit up their armor.

Brian remained dangling in the air, his muscles shaking, his mind wanting to cry out. He could hear the shuffling footsteps stepping past the rope. He hoped and waited. Soon the sound died off and it appeared they had not seen them. His arms ached but he didn't move, waiting until he knew it was safe. The last knight looked back and yelled, Hurry up! Pug, if you can't walk any faster we'll roll ya!"

The chubby knight struggled to keep up with the pace. "I'm a comin', I'm a comin'," he said, panting as he made his way up the path. The rest of the knights followed a curve in the path around a jutting rock and were gone. As the fat knight struggled to make the climb, he took off his spiked helmet. He mopped dripping perspiration from his face with a dirty rag. He moved sluggishly over to where the rope lay covered on the path. He stuck the top of his spiked helmet in the dirt and sat on it with an exhausted sigh. He then carelessly tossed his spear in the dirt.

"Come on! Pug!" a far-off voice yelled.

"Right behind ya!" he screamed, hoping to sound closer than he was.

While catching his breath he looked down and noticed part of the exposed rope. He knelt down with the torch and brushed the dirt away. He followed the rope to the edge of the path and looked down. Brian looked up at him, dangling hopelessly.

"Hey! I got 'im! . . . I got him!" the knight bellowed. But it was too late, for now he was too far behind to be heard.

Ebil leaped out from behind the rock, cackling like a madman. The knight turned toward Ebil wide eyed. "Huh?" choked the knight. He thrust his helmet up to block Ebil's hard slashing blow. The knight dove for his spear but was quickly chopped down.

He tried clumsily to roll out of Ebil's reach but Ebil followed, hacking away at him. Dented and exhausted, the pudgy knight hit his head and lay motionless on the dusty path.

Tommy and Cassie climbed down from the rocks and went to the edge of the path to see if Brian was still holding on.

"Are you okay?" Tommy asked. "Can you make it up?"

"I think so!" Brian gasped. He grunted and began pulling himself up on the rope. Veins stood out on his arms and warm sweat rolled off his face, stinging his eyes.

Cassie and Tommy felt each stretch of his arms that brought Brian closer to them and further away from death. Straining with every movement, Brian painfully moved near the top of the rope.

Tommy reached down for his brother. Brian stretched out his sweaty hand; his fingers quivering for a moment, then Tommy grabbed his wrist. Cassie pulled on his arm, dragging his fatigued body over the edge.

Tommy looked up and saw the dented knight standing over him.

"What?" Tommy screamed.

The knight pulled off his helmet to reveal Ebil's face. "What do you think?" Ebil asked, posing grandly.

"What are you doing?" asked Tommy.

"I'm not going in gargon land without armor," he replied.

"They're going to be coming back for Puggo," Cassie said as she looked at the knight lying there in his dirty long underwear.

"Tom, take his spear," said Brian regaining his composure.

The knight began regaining consciousness as Ebil pulled the last bit of armor off his foot. Tommy grabbed the knight's spear. The knight groggily sat up. "What? Uh . . . What are you gonna do with me?" he whined.

"Why, feed you to the mountain air," Ebil growled as he stared coldly into him.

"No . . . please I . . . I'm, I mean I wasn't after you. I just do as I'm told."

Ebil pointed his crooked finger at the trembling knight. "Those who lie are afraid of the truth."

"I didn't come to hurt you . . . I really don't care . . . I'd much rather be feasting."

"I bet you would!" Brian sneered.

A little smile began to form at the corners of Pug's mouth. "I know what you are up to! You were always so smart. While the Knights went over the mountain you were doubling back to the castle. Clever . . . I'll do anything you want Cassie. Just don't let them toss me off this mountain."

"Pug, you spineless fish," Cassie snapped, "I don't need any help from you! You were always acting so tough while I was growing up and now look at you. All you are is a fat phony."

"Help! Don't hurt me! Please!!" Pug bellowed.

Brian nudged Cassie. "They will be coming back to look for him."

"Pug . . ." said Cassie, "You can go now; go on!"

"What? Huh?" he said, still sitting in the dirt.

"Go on Jumbo, get lost!"

"Oh . . . uh okay. Thank you . . . um . . ." Pug jumped up and thundered up the path away from them.

"Brian." Said Cassie. "We'd better hide again. They'll come back, you know. He thinks we're doubling back to the castle. Which makes sense when you think about it. No one in their right mind would go over the mountain. There are miles and miles of rocks to hide in and in the dark I doubt if even Leether could find us."

Brian agreed, so the four began looking for a place to hide. They crawled between the large jutting stones.

When they all settled in, Brian realized Cassie and he were hidden behind the same rock slab.

"I was here first," he thought. "How come she hid up here right next to me? There are plenty of other places to hide. I wonder if she likes me?" The moonlight gave her face a warm appealing glow. "Boy, is she pretty . . ." he thought. He wanted to hold her, to tell her his inner most feelings and thoughts, but first he wanted her to like him. "She's been changing," he thought. "She trusts me more now. She's been acting nicer."

He thought of sliding his arm around her waist. "How nice that would be, but what would she do? Would she like it or would she scream? Do I dare?" He moved his arm toward her, and then in a moment of panic folded it cautiously in front of him.

"What are you doing?" she whispered. He could feel her soft breath on his face and felt as if he were going to melt.

"Shhh," he replied. "I . . . I think I hear them coming already."

The chubby knight's obnoxious voice pierced the darkness. "I think it goes with out saying that I fought very bravely, all four at once. They will not want to mess with Pug again!"

"Enough!" The priest growled. Leether raised his hands to the clear night sky. "Justice must be done for Nimbus!"

Brian glanced at Cassie who shuddered silently; Brian could clearly see she was in fear of the man.

"What is it about him that makes her so scared?" he thought.

Leether began to chant and a foggy reddish orange mist seeped from the round knob on the end of his twisted scepter.

"Vapor, vapid . . . the smaze a spirtless brume nepheloid and moribund!" He paused then shouted into the heavens, "Dissolutin and carmine coronach! . . ."

His words echoed, lingering in Brian's mind.

"Pug's lying!" said a knight "He couldn't keep up so he made this up. He was hot so he wanted an excuse to take off his armor and have us wait for him."

"Not true!" Pug protested "We fought right here. I'm sure I speared one or two of em. They're tricksters; they were going to double back down the path toward the castle."

Leether turned to his men. "We will move back down the path toward the castle. By first morning light we'll see their tracks more clearly and know where they have or have not been!" The priest glared at the pudgy knight, who sheepishly looked down at his bare, stubby toes.

The priest and knights quickly moved back down the path and out of sight.

Cassie whispered, "This should buy us some time. If we hurry, maybe we can be on the other side of the mountain by morning. It's been said it gets cold in the mountains at night, so it's best if we keep moving."

Guided by moonlight, Brian led them along the path through the penetrating cold that enveloped them. Sparse foliage grew here and there and was covered with a thin coating of ice.

Chapter Five

Frost had formed on Ebil's dented armor. Tommy rubbed his hands together and shivered. "We'd die up here if we fell asleep," he said. "It's so cold!"

"If we just keep moving," said Brian, "we'll be all right."

The wind at his back, Ebil spoke hoarsely as he strode along in the cold breeze. "The cold . . . crisp and thin, it attacks me with needles and pins. Icy death I feel as the chill cracks my face. It stings and numbs and reminds me of my place. As the wind blasts off the frozen branches, it puts me again in mindless trances. How dull and dim and silent it grows, when the cold has touched my soul!!"

"Crisp and thin . . ." said Tommy. They walked wearily hour by hour, into the night. They kept moving because they all knew what was behind them. The air became warmer as they descended, leaving the altitudes. Leafy green foliage thrived along the path and between the rocks and crevices.

"It can't be long till daybreak," said Brian.

His words snapped Ebil out of his walking trance. "In a small slice of time the light will spill over into the dark and the moist scent of dew and the crisp morning air will surround us."

"We need to rest," Cassie suggested limply. They all followed her lead and sat down in the flowering foliage. Within minutes and without any forethought, all had drifted into a much-needed sleep.

Chapter Six

The Party

Ebil woke in the late morning to a bright sun. His face was moist and his mouth dry. He lay inside the hot black armor, which felt like being inside a small black stove.

Ebil contemplated sitting up. "Hmm," he said. He listened to his voice inside the helmet and liked its deep vibrating sound. Ebil began talking out loud, enjoying the varying pitches of his own voice. "Why, who are you?" he asked himself deeply, gesturing with his hands. "Why, I'm Ebil J. Yabut." He lay on his back amused. He tried gurgling noises, then did a few good bubbling swamp imitations.

He finally sat up, then made more noises as his eyes drifted over the dewy leaves and across the shadowy path to where his friends lay asleep. At first he was surprised that his gurgling hadn't awakened them.

"They still aren't home yet," he thought. "Hello?" he said quietly. "Is anyone at home?"

Brian opened one eye, keeping the other closed to protect it from the rising sun. "Mornin' Ebe," he said smiling.

"Afternoon," Ebil replied, cocking his head to one side. "Raven . . . Cassie and Tommy aren't home yet!"

Brian grinned. "Well, have you tried knocking on their door?"

"Of course!" Ebil muttered. "Should have thought of it." He leaned forward and rapped his knuckles against their sleeping heads.

"Knock, knock."

"Hey!" said Tommy, startled.

"Who is it?" Cassie said sweetly.

"You weren't sleeping," Brian said, pointing an accusing finger at her.

"I overheard you," she giggled.

Ebil began talking to himself as he climbed to his feet. "Short? I am . . . but on which end?"

Brian shook his head. "You're something else . . . but what else I haven't a clue!"

Ebil took off the hot helmet and tossed it carelessly into the brush. "The helmet still wears the scent of its former owner," he said. "Pugo's presence still lingers."

Tommy giggled.

Brian licked his finger and held it up. "The wind is blowing this way," he said, pointing at the forest a short distance from the base of the mountain.

The sun was warm and the air crisp. Blotchy red clouds hung on the distant horizon. They reminded Brian of the Nimbus priest who wouldn't rest until he found them.

They moved down the mountain slope and entered the dense forest. It was overgrown with huge leafy plants and monstrous twisted trees bearing strange fruit.

"Look," Cassie said as she plucked an oblong purple fruit from a thorny bush and bit eagerly into it. "Purple Pozz." She handed one to Brian. He examined it as the others watched and then took a bite, feeling the sweet warm taste fill his mouth.

"Mmmm, not bad."

"I know which roots and fruit are okay to eat," said Cassie. She gathered a variety of roots and berries, which they ate with relish.

Their meal was interrupted, however, by a blast of cold air that spun around them, hissing. "Thissss waay," It blew through the trees, whistling and hissing as it went.

"Are you sure this is a friendly spirit we're following?" Cassie asked.

"Well," Brian paused, "uh, it brought me here, gave me my brother," he said, placing his arm on Tommy's shoulder, "and saved my life."

"Yeah," Tommy agreed.

"Have you asked yourself why?" said Ebil, bugging out his eyes. "It's probably some moon-struck wizard who eats heads."

"I doubt it," said Brian.

"Judge yourself by others," said Ebil, "or is it never judge others by yourself, but why? Why? Why?" he said, clutching his head as if going mad. "Is a Raven like a writing desk?"

Brian shook his head, and then walked into the maze of bushes and trees. The air was bittersweet and alive with sounds of busy little animals. But Brian sensed there was a real danger here. He could feel it. He stepped cautiously through the leafy plants. His eyes darted as he brushed back the foliage with the sword.

"Brian, come here, look at this," said Tommy. Brian walked back to where his brother stood. Tommy was pointing at a small lizard crawling calmly along a low branch. Brian assumed it was his seeing this familiar creature that had sparked Tommy's interest. But actually Tommy was looking at a flower blossom, which grew off the same branch.

"It's kinda pretty. I would pick it for Ma, if I knew we were going to see her again," he said. The flower blossom snapped out like a cobra and the lizard was gone.

"Ah!" Tommy stumbled back horrified. "I don't . . . I don't like this place. It gives me the creeps."

"Makes the skin crawl," said Ebil.

Cassie spoke up, sounding like a mother. "I tried to warn you that it's dangerous over here!"

"Well, I'm not afraid!" Tommy announced. They all stared at him with his new found courage.

Ebil grinned. "You mean you're afraid to admit it?"

Then ground shook with a loud boom! Leaves and branches fell from the trees. Boom . . . Boom.

"It's an earthquake!" Brian screeched, diving toward the roots of a huge tree.

"No! No! No!" Ebil panted, tumbling over backward next to Brian. Cassie took Tommy by the hand and they fell toward the tree next to Brian and Ebil.

"What is it?" Brian yelled.

"It's," Cassie began.

"A gargon," Ebil finished for her.

Cassie tried to shriek but the sound never escaped her lips.

They all lay very still. Brian could see the gargon approach. It was everything they had said it was, and even bigger than the ones at the castle.

He could hear the beast panting as it moved closer, stomping, clawing and sniffing. There were flickering reflections of trees, in its glossy black eyes. It stomped right by the foursome in search of who knows what . . . a meal perhaps?

"It's gone," Cassie whispered softly, opening her eyes.

Relieved that they were still alive, Brian wanted to give Cassie a kiss in celebration, but held back. "Uh . . . yeah, it was huge," he replied.

"Gigantic," Tommy stammered.

"A stompin', snortin' nightmare," Ebil slurred with a weed dangling from the corner of his mouth. Ebil noticed Tommy was listening intently. "Do you have nightmares Tommy?" he asked as they got back to their feet.

"Yeah, real bad ones."

"Do they frighten you?"

"Yeah, sometimes."

Ebil took the spear they had taken from the knight and planted it firmly in the soil. "Don't be afraid of imagined horrors. There are plenty of real ones around here to take their place."

"Is that supposed to make him feel better?" smiled Brian

Ebil's voice became raspy and the sun lit up his eyes as he spoke. "Fear caused by the unknown, you feel it when you're alone. What is this thing that haunts your brain, gives you nightmares and mental strain? I know it's inside your head, but why does it come out when you're in bed? You must challenge these unseen creatures with their imagined evil minds and hideous features. Otherwise they will take hold and haunt you until you get old and cold. If you imagine something that scares you . . . all you have to do is imagine something that will protect you from what you imagined that scares you."

"Sometimes you make sense," Tommy assured him.

"It's like playing with needles and pins," said Ebil.

"And the rest of the time you talk in riddles," said Brian.

"Where do you get all those rhymes from?" Tommy asked.

"Well," said Ebil, "when I see one floating, I just pluck it out of the air."

Tommy nodded.

They began to move between the shadowed trees. Brian watched how the moving leaves and branches made glittering patterns across the ground. It was more peaceful now that the danger seemed to have passed.

Cassie turned to Brian as they strolled together through the rustling leaves. "Tell me where you're from," she asked quietly.

"Another world," he answered.

"How did you get here?"

"Through a hole in a pond. I know it sounds stupid but that's how it happened. You speak the same language, so I think it must have happened to others throughout the years."

"I've been watching you," she said. "You're different. You certainly aren't from around here. And you want to follow this voice in the breeze because you think it can get you back through that pond to home, right?"

"Right!"

"I wish I knew where I was going," she said, looking down while kicking up the leaves.

"Just stick with us something will work out," he said.

Cassie's mouth gave way to a small smile, which Brian caught from the corner of his eye.

"Cassie?" he asked.

"Yes?"

"Do you still believe in that red cloud?"

"I . . . I don't know anymore. It's been ceremonies and sacrifices all my life and no one ever questioned it . . . until you came along."

Ebil interjected as usual. "See things from all sides. Shallow mindedness is next to blindness. Some need the threat of darkness to make them good, the wise need only the strength within themselves. Life will reflect back to you all the good or bad you do."

"Did you pluck that out of the air?" Cassie asked.

"No," Ebil cackled. "It was in your mind all the time."

They walked all day through the woods, until the curtain of darkness began to fall slowly around them.

The sun disappeared and was replaced by two pale blue moons one large, one smaller and darker. The small one moved like a minute hand through the sky while the large one remained still. Brian stared in wonderment as the little moon disappeared behind the big one. "It must be rotating," he muttered.

"What?" Tommy asked.

"Uh . . ." Brian pointed at the sky.

"Their moon has a moon."

"Hmm."

"Leether says the small moon is magical because it can disappear," said Cassie.

"Only from view," Ebil remarked.

"The small one just moves behind the big one," said Brian.

"But why would it do that? Oh, I guess anything's possible," she said, not truly convinced.

Brian's eyes strained as he plunged through the dark unknown of the forest. They moved slowly and smoothly between the trees, as did the breeze. A dark stillness seemed to follow them through the woods.

"The quiet!" Ebil whispered sharply. "Listen . . . It's so deafening, I can hear my very thoughts." He clutched his head and his knobby fingers dug into his scrambled hair. "I'm thinking what I'm thinking, and I'm thinking about what I'm thinking, I'm thinking."

Tommy wanted to help his troubled friend. "Don't think about it!" he said quietly.

"But when I think about not thinking about it, I am in fact thinking about it!"

"Then . . ." Tommy paused, "quit trying not to think about it, and your mind will eventually get bored and move on to other things."

Ebil grinned and patted Tommy on the back. "You have some hidden depths in your mind's sea."

Tommy grinned.

They walked up to a small hill that had a faint yellow glow coming from the other side.

"Shhhh," said Cassie grabbing Brian's arm. "I hear faint voices, strange, growling ones."

"I can hear it too," Tommy whispered, looking at the hill. "It's coming from over there," he said.

Ebil fidgeted with an old leaf. "It comes from the glow," he gurgled. "Many, many flickering tongues."

"Well, let's check it out!" said Brian laying the sword across his shoulder.

"Why?" Cassie asked.

"Because I'm curious," he replied. "If you don't want to come, take the spear from Ebil. Tommy can stay with you. Me and Ebil won't be long so just stay put."

"Okay," she nodded, "but it might be safer if we don't know what it is."

Tommy frowned. "Aw, come on, she'll be all right . . . Let me come."

Brian glared at his pouting brother.

Tommy got the unspoken message. "I'll stay!" he said reluctantly.

Brian laid the flat edge of the sword across his shoulder as the two of them walked toward the hill. The blue moons reflected and slid down Ebil's dented armor.

"Be careful," Cassie said, feeling her advise might some how protect them.

As Brian and Ebil climbed the hill the eerie sounds became clearer and stronger. Near the top they layed down and pulled themselves up to look over on the other side. They could see a large clearing below them.

Some kind of hideous party was going on. There were about a hundred nasty, two-legged, tailed beasts. Most of them had scales, puckering muscles, rows of razor sharp teeth and flickering tongues. They appeared to be about eight feet tall. They had spikes and facial features like an ugly horned toad.

A blasting fire roared up from a deep pit in the center of the clearing. Some drooling monsters tossed things into the disintegrating flames, as others chanted, panted and then danced away from the fire.

Some fought each other to steal each other's lives away, while being poked by onlookers with sharpened sticks.

Brian and Ebil watched motionless, for quite awhile, just watching. Brian was horrified when the onlookers devoured the loser of one of the fights and the leftovers were tossed in the flames as others chanted.

"Oh my God!" he whispered to Ebil. "Did you see that?"

Ebil giggled. "Think they're friendly?"

Suddenly Brian felt the presence of another, the feeling of eyes boring into him. He heard the faint sound of rustling leaves. He froze, his heart pounding in anticipation. Finally he dared to look.

His worst fears were realized with the turn of his head.

A seething, frothing monster towered over them holding a long sickle. Brian gasped as the muscles of the horrible thing twitched and quivered like a snake ready to strike. They lay pinned down, afraid to move.

"Did somebody lose a nightmare?" Ebil asked.

"What now?" whispered Brian. "By the time I bring the sword around, one of us will be cut in half."

The monster hissed, his tongue flickering like a flame from his jaws. The beast pulled the weapon back to bring it down with the full force of its body. Ebil rolled out of the way and Brian reached helplessly for the sword. In the same instant a spear zipped through the scaled thing's middle and poked out its beastly chest. The thing let out an ear-piercing scream. "Ssssarah! Ssssaarah!" It tried to pull the spear from its pulsating thorax, stumbled violently, then stopped and stood motionless for a moment before falling lifelessly to the ground.

Brian saw Cassie and Tommy standing in the shadows behind where the creature lay.

"What are you doing here?" Brian asked.

"We got worried and came looking for you," she said.

"Well, uh . . . nice shot!"

"They're coming up the hill after us!" Ebil yelled.

The foursome ran down the hill, crashing through the brush and maze of overgrown twisted trees.

"I hope we can outrun them!" Brian yelled between panting breaths. Devilish hell-cries shattered the night as hoards of mutated creatures spilled over the hill charging at them.

"We're gonna get caught! We're really gonna!" Tommy sucked in the night air and could feel it burning in his throat. His small legs pumped and pushed and gave up, but then kept going. Still the beasts came growling nearer. He could picture their bumpy bodies and open groping jaws filled with sharp teeth and steamy saliva. "We're gonna get it!" he cried.

"What was, will always be," Ebil howled through the noise of thrashing leaves. "What will be will never come to pass."

Brian turned, slowing slightly. "Come on, up in the tree, come on! It's our only chance!" He jumped and grabbed a heavy vine that wound around the trunk, then pulled himself up with one arm as he waved his friends on.

The tree was well chosen. It was big and winding with stocky branches holding big shiny emerald-green leaves. Vines wound around it like fat snakes, making for excellent climbing. In a few moments they were all hidden along the mammoth branches. They peeked every now and then when they dared, but mostly listened.

But those hideous hell-worshipping beasts never came. Where were they? Brian could hear them growling and groping, but the sound wasn't getting louder or closer.

"Something funny is going on," Cassie whispered. Brian picked his head up off the smooth branch and moved for a better view.

"They're . . . they're fighting someone else," he said, trying to see better.

"Who? Cassie asked.

Chapter Six

"It looks like . . . It is! It's Leether! They're fighting Leether! He must have been right behind us and now they've got 'im!"

"Don't count him out," Cassie whispered. "He has power. He has unknown powers."

"Unknown even to him," Brian grinned.

The Black Knights stood in a circle, swords extended and ready for battle. Leether stood in the center of the circle, showing no fear as the beasts taunted, clawed and thrust strange weapons at them. As the beasts moved in for the kill, Leether began to chant. His voice carried into the night sky. He pushed his black, winding staff into the air as dense red mist steeped out of the end and hung in the air above him.

Brian had to chuckle at the uselessness of Leether's dramatics. Then a chill ran down his back when he realized what horror they would witness.

The beasts swarmed in clawing and biting. The knights fought bravely but were forced back and cut down quickly as their circle became smaller and smaller. The crimson red haze hanging in the air sunk to the ground and around the circle of knights as Leether's chanting grew more intense.

When the haze sank into the earth around the knights it quickly transformed the ground into a quicksand like muck. The muck acted like a moat protecting Leether and the knights. Unafraid the monsters aggressively moved in to cross it.

The hellish creatures dug and clawed, sinking slowly into the gurgling ooze around the knights. Other creatures backed out of the sticky moat but continued taunting.

The monsters, drooling and tasting a kill, were unshaken as they clawed and swung crude sickle like weapons across the moat at the knights.

Leether, who was building up into a chanting frenzy, yelled out, "Red miasma open up the boggy moor, set free the headless biodae vipers and take these creatures back to hell."

Instantly, red smoke burst from the bubbling slime. Long, wide snake-like things squirmed out of the gurgling ooze. Winding and dripping with gook, they reached like tentacles for the beasts. The monsters fought them eagerly, chopping off chunks of tentacles and wrestling them into the muck. Tentacles continued to grow out of the slime, overpowering the hideous demons. These tentacles wrapped like boa constrictors around the monsters, pulling them down forever into the mucky depths.

"His power is in that staff," Cassie whispered.

"Let's get outa here now!" Brian urged. "I've seen enough."

"It's now or forever," Ebil gurgled. They silently climbed down from the tree and scurried into the woods, ever conscious of what they left behind and what could have been.

Chapter Seven

A Taste of Infinity

The next day they walked out of the dense forest and into a sparsely wooded area. The ground was covered with a soft blanket of grass and cool moss. The trees were large but were spaced farther apart. Smooth round boulders lay here and there in the sunlit grasses.

"Nice place for a picnic," smiled Cassie as she walked out of the brush and into the clearing.

Tommy ran ahead and rolled in the spongy grass. "This feels good!" he said. "Like home."

Brian chuckled and stuck his sword in the ground. "It does? Well, let me try!" he said, charging at his brother. Running at full speed, he put his palms to the ground and went into a forward roll. As he flipped, his heavy foot caught Tommy on the top of the head.

"Hey!" Tommy yelled, holding his scalp. "Watch where you're going!"

Brian snickered. "Watch where you're laying!"

"Oh yeah?" said Tommy, sitting up.

"Yeah!" laughed Brian.

Tommy lunged at Brian, pouncing on him like some great cat. They struggled and tumbled in the grass.

Brian flipped Tommy over his shoulder and tried to force-feed him a handful of grass, as he straddled him.

"Help!" Tommy yelled. "Get 'im off me! Cassie! Ebe! Get 'im off me."

Ebil looked at Cassie.

"Let's get 'im!" she grinned. Ebil grunted and nodded, quickly tossing off his clumsy armor. Together they ran to Tommy's aid.

"Get 'im! Get 'im!" Tommy burst, trying to yell and at the same time spit the grass out of his mouth. Cassie and Ebil jumped on Brian's back, flattening him on top of Tommy. "Puha!"

Brian rolled around wrestling the three of them. He found Ebil to be the strongest so he directed most of his attention to him.

Ebil giggled insanely. "Huh, ha! Uhmummaaahaa." As Cassie hung on Brian's back, Tommy twisted his brother's foot.

"Ow! Quit it!" Brian cried. Tommy giggled, then stripped off Brian's shoe and tickled the bottom of his foot as Brian squirmed and kicked.

The torture was more than he could stand. "Ha, ha . . . come on, quit . . . ha, ha . . . it." His laughter weakened him enough that Ebil was able to force him to the ground. The others piled on.

"I give! I give!" he stammered. "You win! You won!"

Tommy laughed in victory and rolled off the pile.

"Don't mess with me no more, Brian!"

Ebil fell off and rolled up into a handstand to look at the world upside down. "Everything looks much clearer now," he chuckled.

Cassie giggled and remained sitting on Brian. "Maybe you should stay that way," she said.

"Uh . . . . Cassie?" said Tommy. "Aren't you gonna get off him?"

"Uh? Oh!" she said, embarrassed, she got to her feet, suddenly feeling self-conscious.

Brian smiled and put his hands behind his head, gazing at the fluffy white clouds. "This place kinda reminds me of home," he said.

"Burrr," shivered Ebil, the sun glancing off his head.

"How can you be so cold?" Cassie asked.

"I can feel the chill of a cold heart," he said as he rubbed his arms.

"What?" Brian asked, confused.

"I can feel something's here. My eyes cannot find it but in my mind I know they're here."

"Who?" Brian asked, sitting up and looking around.

"Can't you feel it?" Ebil yelped, "It's . . . it's all around us . . . hatred, terrible hatred, spawned by fear, confusion made right by dissolution. Shallow minds made to walk fine lines, venting frustration upon those of their own creation!"

Tommy rolled over. "Brian, what's he talking about?"

Brian shrugged his shoulders as Ebil continued.

"They live like blind men, not knowing where they're going or where they've been. Those who can see out, but have no perspective in."

"But I'm not blind, madman," said a stern icy voice.

"Who's there?" Brian called out. They couldn't see where the voice came from.

Then a dark shape stepped out from behind a tree as if appearing out of nowhere.

"Huh!" Cassie gasped.

"Boppity . . . Bop!" said Ebil smiling. "Is it him?" Ebil asked, "or is he just a figment of my imagination?"

"It's Leether!" Brian answered.

"Maybe he's imagining us?" said Ebil, shoving his knobby hands into his face and pushing his skin around.

"Let's take 'im," Brian whispered just loud enough to be heard.

A dozen dark warriors stepped out from behind the trees and boulders surrounding them.

"Uh . . . forget it . . ." Brian mumbled.

"The ceremony shall begin!" rejoiced Leether. The knights ran over and roughly grabbed them. The four were dragged to a mossy tree and sat up against it.

Brian realized these could be his last breaths . . . his last thoughts. He could faintly hear Tommy sobbing as their hands were tied together behind their backs, and then around the same large tree.

Brian turned to look at Cassie's sweet face. She stared ahead, not moving, not crying.

"We should have tried to run!" Brian shouted in despair.

A chubby, overweight knight wearing only his long johns walked past Ebil.

"Nice outfit, Pug!" Ebil gurgled.

"What!" the knight stammered. "Hey, is that my armor lying on the ground?"

"Uh . . . may life always be as good to you as you have been to me." The knight sighed, and then stepped back to give Leether room.

"Justice must be done!" the priest kept saying, as if he was trying to convince everyone. He busily built a small fire. In minutes he had a bubbling pot of stinky brew. He chanted strange verses as little balls of glowing smoke rose rapidly from the flames.

"What's he going to do?" Brian asked.

"Send us to infinity," said Ebil.

"Where?" Tommy asked.

"Uh . . ." Ebil thought for a moment. "A place that has no where or when, no dawn or dusk, no past no future, no here or there nor anywhere . . . but everywhere. Too vast to appear in the mind, it stretches on like the end of time. It's no place and every place, an immenseness of open space. Forever, for always, for us . . . everything and nothing."

"Gelidity requiem," the priest mumbled, pulling a ladle of red potion out of the fire. He sniffed it and a brief smile spread across his lips, then he hissed like an angry serpent. His face reddened and swelled as if a fire was burning within him. "Brumous rufecent." Slightly dazed, he staggered toward Tommy.

"Now it's time," said Leether, "today is judgment day."

"It's not my time!" Tommy cried.

"Quiet, little one," smiled Leether as he pulled a twisted dagger from his belt. He pushed the jagged blade snuggly against Tommy's neck, then lifted the steaming ladle to his mouth.

"Drink or I'll open your throat," he whispered softly.

Tommy drank nervously. "Ack!"

Leether worked his way around the tree, kneeling as he forced them all to drink. He poured the bubbly red blend into Brian's mouth. Brian held it there not swallowing. Leether stood, then turned away as Brian let the bitter brew dribble slowly out of the corner of his mouth. Still, almost instantly he could feel it take effect as he became increasingly dazed and lethargic. He could hear a flute playing in rising and falling pitches that seemed to wind through the smoke-filled air.

The priest pulled a brown woven sack over Brian's head while Ebil said, "Reality and dreams, here's where they differ; in reality the rules are stiffer." Brian could feel the bitter foaming potion fizzing in his mouth and its smell hung in the air.

The bag over his head was all he could see. This seemed to be his world now. The threads were loosely woven and light peeked between them. He could hear Leether chanting and the words fizzed in the buzzing of his head.

"Nimbus!" cried the priest, his words flowing off the tip of his pointed tongue. "The grim shall intercede and do justice. He shall lead them to the land of infinity on a spiritless journey, so you may hunger no more."

"Wind!" yelled Brian, becoming numb. "Save us, stop this! Where are you? Spirit in the wind?" He could hear the breezes rustling in the trees, but no whispers. Brian listened hopelessly . . .

Leether continued to rant and Brian could hear him moving back and forth. "Refecent phantom, ghostlike brume . . ." Leether continued.

Brian's watery eyes became firmly fixed on the woven threads of the sack that covered his head. The threads become clearer and clearer and everything else was melting away in a soft haze of words and numb sensations.

He was escaping into the small world of the burlap bag. He felt as if he was very small and the bag was hundreds of feet high. It was as if his mind had somehow become separated from his body and was floating out of his eyes, drifting deep into the vast openness of the bag.

Chapter Seven

Weightless he drifted, tumbling smoothly away toward the outer reaches of the bag. He drifted up to the threads of the burlap bag. The threads were the size of poles, weaving in and out of each other with square spaces in between. Picking up momentum, he glided between the threads and sailed out of the bag into a world of black nothingness. He could still hear Leether's words rumbling into infinity: "The land of the dead . . . rufous smaze a delicate haze."

He could see three faint objects coming out of the distant darkness. They were all headed to the same point in space. As they neared, he could see they were Ebil, Cassie, and Tommy.

"Are we dead yet?" he wondered. They all began rotating, caught up in a current, that carried them slowly round and round.

The Nimbus Priest appeared in the vast reaches of nothingness. He was miles high, his image curving around them as if he were on the outside of a crystal ball looking in at them. He chanted, his words vibrating endlessly into space. "Take them . . ." he cried, "They are yours . . . Take them now!"

Then they heard an old woman's voice sounding, very disturbed, "No! You mustn't!" The priest looked stunned.

"No! No! No!" she screamed with tremendous force. "No!!"

A terrible blast shook the darkness. Brian could feel a powerful shock wave as Leether was blasted into the darkness. Tumbling and screaming, further and further until he disappeared completely . . . into the black nothingness.

Brian woke next to the tree and felt he had been sleeping for some time. At first he didn't know whether he had dreamed the nightmare or if it had really happened. He looked around: there were no knights, no priest just his friends waking up.

"That old lady," Tommy mumbled, wiping his eyes. "She sounded like Grandma."

"Whoever it was, she saved us," Brian said, still slightly dazed.

"Look," said Cassie. "Leether's staff!" She picked it up out of the grass and examined its twisted black shaft.

"Get rid of it!" Ebil warned.

"No!" Cassie said, gritting her teeth. "We may need it!"

Brian tried to reason with her. "But we don't know how to use it; we could get hurt."

"We're keeping it," she said, settling the issue and chapter.

Chapter Eight
Gerbits and Toadstools

The four set off once more, walking through the dreary forest as darkness closed around them. Gloomy trees towered over them. Branches extended like big arms, looking like giant leafy monsters ready to swoop down at any moment.

Then they heard a low, lumbering noise. It sounded like something huge had propelled the sound with immense force.

"What was that?" Tommy whispered.

"Why a melancholy rumble," Ebil said hoarsely.

"Whose?" Brian asked.

"It must have been someone's," Ebil explained.

The trees seemed to close in behind them blocking their exit, as they walked cautiously through the forest. Then they heard it again. It was louder this time.

"There it is again!" Tommy whispered frantically. Cassie held Brian's arm for security.

"Where's it coming from?" she asked.

"I think over there," he said pointing toward the darkened trees.

They continued into the depths of the forest as their imaginations ran wild.

Brian saw something. Barely visible were two small caverns of identical size next to each other behind the trees. Apprehensively, they moved closer and the trees gave way for a better view. He could feel rhythmic pulses of warm, smelly air sailing in and out of the caves.

"What is it?" Cassie asked, still clutching tightly to Brian's arm.

"I don't know," he said softly, "It smells like old socks."

Then the caves appeared to move slightly, to twitch, and a loud rumble came grinding out of the inner depths of the caverns.

All four jumped and all eyes fixed on the origin of the rumble. They peered into the blackness. To their amazement, two glossy black moons rose slowly over the caverns. The moons had darker slits in the center.

"What is it?" Tommy asked.

"Uh . . . gargon!" Cassie yelled.

A rumbling sigh came from the great beast as it picked up its huge head. This startled them so that they ran, ran in a panic fast and hard.

The scaled monster rolled slowly over on its side like a big dog and laid its huge head down in the soft moss.

So relieved was Brian at the gargon's lack of ambition that he stopped running and laughed aloud.

"Oh jeeze, I don't believe it," Brian puffed,

"What a lazy!" Tommy exclaimed.

Cassie spoke up. "I thought he was kinda cute. Maybe he's a nice gargon. If there is such a thing."

"That didn't even cross my mind," Ebil interjected, "not even diagonally."

"He musta just finished eating somebody," Tommy said.

"Must be full," Ebil cackled.

Cassie laid Leether's magic staff casually cross her shoulder. Brian was uneasy about her keeping it. In the dark it almost looked like a black snake with a golden head crawling across her neck. But he knew that to ask her to give it up was pointless because she had been so adamant about keeping it.

They set out once again, moving through the overgrown forest. Brian didn't know why, but the forest was somehow drearier on this night. He could almost hear the silent echoes of lifeless spirits sifting through the leaves. He just wanted to be out of the woods, to feel safe once again.

"I think there's a clearing up ahead," said Tommy when he noticed trees giving away to open spaces. Brian's face lit up.

"Really? I hope so!" he said. They walked out of the woods and into an open field. "We're out of the forest," Brian exclaimed.

"So?" said Cassie.

"Well," said Brian, "I think those woods were giving me claustrophobia."

"What?" Cassie asked.

"I was getting all creeped out back there . . . but I feel better now," he said, looking around with a grin. "I hate the idea of something ugly jumping out at me from behind a tree."

They laid down for the night in the cool green grass as the air rolled lazily around them.

The morning began to warm their slumbering bodies. Brian woke quickly and sat up to survey their surroundings.

Big rolling hills were covered with grass as thick as a shag rug and dotted with millions of toadstools.

Brian rubbed his face. "I'm glad yesterday is over."

"Uh . . ." Ebil squeaked, "the day is gone, but what happened isn't nor will it ever be."

"Huh?" said Brian, amazed that Ebil could be spouting off so early in the morning.

Ebil continued. "Everything you have done builds into what you are. After you have done something, it isn't lost. It will forever be a part of you."

"Thanks, Ebe," Cassie muttered. She began gathering mushrooms for breakfast.

Ebil grinned crookedly, and nodded as if to say, "You're welcome, my pleasure, hope you enjoyed it."

A blustering whirlwind suddenly blew out of the forest, winding around them as a breath of air sang out in its wispy voice, "Follow me . . . Follow me for the key."

Ebil smiled and took off with the wind toward the inviting hills. They laughed and chased him, kicking up mushrooms and shouting. It was a pleasant day with not a red cloud in the sky. They walked, talked, ate mushrooms and told stories. Tommy and Brian taught Cassie a couple of verses of "Here I Go A Wandering," as Ebil hummed along out of key but somehow blending in.

As they journeyed whimsically over the sunken valleys, the toadstools steadily became larger.

Chapter Eight

"Are we shrinking or are they getting bigger," joked Brian as he kicked over a mushroom that came up to his shin.

"Giant white mushrooms," muttered Ebil.

"You mean they get bigger?"

"Harder to eat im, though, when they're so big!" Ebil said this as if it destroyed the thrill.

Brian then walked over the crest of a hill and saw what looked like the tops of thousands of giant white umbrellas. They stood on the top of the hill and stared at an entire forest of mushrooms stretching out for miles. The largest mushrooms were in the middle and near the edge they grew smaller.

"Look at this, will ya!" Brian stammered.

Tommy stood, gazing at mushrooms that were taller than their barn at home.

"Come on!" Cassie smiled, pulling on Brian's arm. "I used to play in the toadstools when I was little. There are some in the woods by the castle . . . did you see them?"

"No, we didn't get around to much sightseeing," he replied.

They ran headlong into the toadstool forest. The ground had no leaves, sticks or grass, just spongy moss that sank eerily with each footstep.

The forest was something out of a dream. Most of the mushrooms were so tall that at eye level you could see only big white soft poles. Overhead, plush white umbrellas blocked out circles of sunlight. The sun peeked through here and there around the white tops. Smaller toadstools grew along the ground but most were so big that Tommy could barely stretch his arms around one.

"Gnort! . . . Snort . . . Grunt! Grunt!"

"What was that?" Brian asked.

Ebil snickered. "There are gerbits in the woods!"

"Gerbits?"

"Ya, mean nasty little beasts they are."

"I don't see 'im!" said Tommy, peering between the toadstools.

"Don't worry," Ebil croaked aloud. "They'll show their horny, thorny little heads."

A small hog waddling like a sleepy cow wandered out from behind a fallen mushroom.

"Snort . . . Snort . . . Gnort!" the pig grumbled, then stopped to stare at them indignantly.

"So that's a gerbit!" Tommy smiled, turning to Brian to see his reaction.

The pig looked fierce with little tusks curving up on each side of his mouth. Hardened bumps started on top of his head and ran down his curved back.

"Snort, snort," said the gerbit as he bobbed his head and trotted at Tommy, grunting with each movement.

"Looks kinda like a razor back hog," said Brian. The boar trotted at Tommy and brushed against his leg.

Tommy dropped the sword from his shoulder and swatted the swine hard on the hind end.

"Snotty little porker," said Tommy as the pig squealed and tucked his twisted tail between his legs and scurried off. Tommy and Brian laughed.

"To have a friend, a man must be one," Ebil cautioned.

"I've got enough pig friends already," said Tommy, bellowing with laughter.

Chapter Eight

Suddenly they heard a deeper grunting, then another and another.

They saw four or five heavy-hoofed gerbits advancing like runaway rapids between the mushrooms.

"Krot!" screamed Cassie. "Everyone scatter!"

Brian took the sword from Tommy and swung wildly as the horned swine charged. He swatted one away with the flat edge of the sword, but the pig stumbled, grunted and charged once again.

Meanwhile, Tommy was chased screeching through mushrooms by a little gerbit. Ebil desperately tried to pull the big female porker off his leg. Cassie shimmied up a mushroom to safety as she had done as a little girl.

Ebil hopped on one leg as Momma porker tugged him away with her teeth.

Tommy had been chased off, and Brian was getting tired.

"This is getting serious," Brian thought to himself. "I've got to do something!"

He turned his sword and exposed the sharp edge of the blade as the nasty gerbit grunted hoarsely and charged headfirst at him. Brian swung the wide blade around in a flash and laid open a deep cut on the pig's hindquarters.

The gerbit tumbled and stumbled off, squealing frantically.

Brian ran over and kicked the big gerbit off Ebil's leg.

"Snort . . . squee" The big pig bounced on his side, then regained his balance and turned to charge. Brian brought his sword back.

The pig stopped as if sizing up Brian, and then in an instant turned and ran for home.

When the ruckus was over, Cassie shimmied down the mushroom. "Where's Tommy," she asked.

"They heard a high squeal"

"I don't know," said Brian, "but I think he's getting closer."

A small porker emerged running through the toadstools with Tommy hot on his heels yelling, "Shoo, shoo pig!" The gerbit ran by them but Tommy held up, out of breath.

"They were getting the best of us for a while," said Brian.

"If they come back, climb a toadstool," Cassie explained. "You've got to be very careful not to upset these gerbits . . ."

The rest of the day was peaceful in comparison. They moved along between the white, pole-like toadstool stems. It was quiet and tranquil. Strangely, not one gerbit was seen, just a few fuzzy little animals scurrying away.

Eventually, the sun began to set and the tranquility gave way to a feeling that someone may be watching them. That eerie fear of the unknown, something out there in the dark of the night, was with them once again.

"Let's wait until tomorrow to go any further," Brian said, glancing behind them.

"Yeah," agreed Tommy. "I hate to walk when we can't see what we're walking into."

"But we're kind of unprotected out here in the open," said Cassie. "Remember those nasty little gerbits."

She looked at the smaller mushrooms, which grew here and there. "I used to roll the fallen mushrooms in a circle and make a fort."

"Splendid!" Ebil shrieked, applauding wildly.

"I'll cut 'im and you stack 'im!" said Brian as he marched over to a shoulder-high toadstool.

"Check!" Ebil hollered, saluting Brian like an obedient soldier.

Brian began cutting down mushrooms while the rest of them rolled the mushrooms neatly into an overlapping circle. The mushroom tops looked like fluffy white shields held closely together.

"I'll sleep much easier now," Cassie said when they had finished. She stepped back to look at their work and was delighted.

"Kinda nice," said Tommy, pushing aside a mushroom and going inside with the rest following.

Brian leaned back against the soft mushroom and put his hands behind his head.

Cassie got some toadstool chunks and started a warm radiant fire in the center of the camp. Brian relaxed and watched in admiration.

"I wish we were home," said Tommy.

"I wonder if we'll ever get back," Brian mumbled as he gazed into the crackling flames.

As the moons rose high in the heavens, shadows seemed to crawl across the ground under their own power.

"Brian," Tommy said, "what if we're really dead? What if we drowned in that pond?"

Ebil laughed fiendishly. "Then you can't get back, can you?!"

"Well," said Brian, "this sure ain't heaven." He glanced at Cassie, making eye contact, and continued. "And it sure ain't hell."

Ebil's eyes twinkled and he grinned his toothy grin. "What is it like after we die? No one knows except those who try."

Cassie shook her head at Ebil and grinned.

Ebil went on. "The years go by one by one, and after they're gone then we have none. We go through life trying to live our hopes and dreams, but after we're gone what does it mean? People are funny when they don't know the answer, they make up stories and tales and this is where Nimbus fails." Ebil paused for a moment as if he forgot the ending.

"Is that it?" Brian asked. "Anything else?"

"Uh," Ebil gurgled faintly, "make the world better for those around you. That is your true measure."

"You aren't so crazy," smiled Brian.

"You aren't so crazy," Ebil squawked.

"Hey! This moss is wet over here, shrieked Cassie, jumping up. She danced around brushing off her rump, and then warmed it by the fire.

"Is it wet by you, Brian?"

Brian felt the moss next to him. "Uh . . . no, I mean I don't think so," he answered politely.

"Good," she said smiling and strutted over to him. She plopped down so close to him that he had to move to one side.

Brian stared at the twisted black staff she was holding. She noticed it made him uncomfortable, so she tossed it near the fire.

Brian was feeling self-conscious sitting so close to Cassie when there was obviously so much extra room elsewhere. Observing this, Tommy made faces at Brian, every time Cassie wasn't looking, to embarrass him.

"I wonder if the moss was really wet?" Brian thought to himself. "I bet she just wanted an excuse to sit by me or . . . maybe it was wet. She's so close, she could have sat further away." He stared at her smooth face and watched the firelight flicker against her shiny black hair.

She turned her head to look at him. His eyes darted, and he hoped she didn't notice he had been staring.

"What do I do now?" he thought. "I wanna kiss and hug her and tell her I like her. I'd probably scare her if I tried . . . I think she likes me, but what if she doesn't . . . I can't just kiss her out of the blue. I'll start a conversation."

"Um, Cassie, are you more comfortable now?"

She smiled sweetly. "Yeah," she answered.

"That conversation didn't last so long," he thought, "but she smiled. She smiled at me really nice."

He glanced across the fire and saw that Ebil and Tommy were dozing off.

"Are you cold?" Brian asked.

"Um . . . yeah, I am, kinda, can I scooch over a little bit to keep warm?" she asked.

Brian nodded, not believing she had suggested it. As she slid over, he pulled his arm up, intending to place it gently around her shoulder. His timing was off and his elbow smashed her hard in the ear.

"Ow!" she cried out, holding her wounded head.

"I'm sorry," he said, "I didn't mean to!"

Ebil and Tommy woke up, startled. "What's going on?" Tommy asked.

"I hit Cassie in the head," Brian said bluntly.

"How come . . . what'd she do?"

"She didn't do anything!"

"Then why did you hit her?"

"Go back to sleep" Brian ordered. Tommy rolled over and closed his eyes. Brian whispered to Cassie, "Is it okay?"

She moved her hand and he could see how red her ear was.

"It doesn't hurt anymore," she said quietly.

"Cassie, I . . ."

"Yes?"

"I really like you a lot . . . I mean, I have for a while."

Her face lit up. "I think you're really sweet, Brian. You've always been so nice . . . um, even when I wasn't."

"I don't believe it; I can't believe this is happening," he thought. He looked into her brown eyes and felt himself drawn closer.

She touched his face, and he gave her the warm kiss he had been dreaming about for a long time.

The fire crackled and they leaned together against the cushy mushroom. They hugged and talked softly until they fell asleep in each other's arms.

Hours later, Brian woke with a start. He glanced around, looking for some reason for his awakening. "It must have been a noise," he thought. He looked into Cassie's sweet sleeping face; Ebil and Tommy were asleep too. He lay back and watched the moons lazily rotate, one around the other.

"Snort."

"What was that?" he wondered. He got up quietly to not to wake the rest of them, and peered over the tops of the curved mushrooms.

There were hundreds of eyes, all lit up by the moonlight. They were everywhere, as many as the stars in the sky. He blinked his tired eyes to assure himself he wasn't hallucinating.

"Who do all these glowing eyes belong to?" he asked himself. "Why are they hiding in the dark? Must be those stupid gerbits! How can there be so many!"

"Hey," Brian whispered. "Wake up! We might be in trouble!"

"What is it?" Tommy asked, with one eye open.

Suddenly the air was filled with snorting, grunting and the trampling of little hooves as the gerbits charged. They rumbled head long into the fort.

In a moment the toadstool refuge they had taken such care to build was torn into flying bits by the raging boars. Cassie clutched the magic staff and tried to protect herself behind a fallen mushroom. Ebil scrambled for the sword amidst the sea of running pigs.

All hell broke loose. Tommy was bumped to his knees, gerbits swarming him like bees to a hive.

"Brian!" he yelled.

Brian, meanwhile, was fighting for his life. He spun around throwing gerbits off his back, just to have more jump on him.

Ebil cut them down with the large sword, but more kept coming.

Cassie, still slightly protected behind the crumbling mushroom, screamed wildly while waving the black scepter in the air. "Nimbus! . . . Help us! Stop them! Cloud, where are you?"

She continued screaming, waiting for the magic from the twisted staff to unveil itself.

The sea of stampeding gerbits cut down Brian's legs and in an instant his face was trampled into the cool moss. All he could see was a forest of gerbit legs. Their hard little hooves dug sharply into his back. He tried to stand but their immense weight kept him pinned to the ground.

Cassie felt gerbits slamming into her legs. Her feet were finally knocked out from under her and she felt herself falling backwards. In a last effort, she threw the staff hard and high into the night sky as she went down.

"Help us!" she screamed, hoping her last breath would somehow be carried with the staff.

The staff sailed slowly, spinning as it climbed high in the sky. Cassie fell into the mass of pigs and was instantly consumed by their trampling hooves. The staff kept climbing as if drawn by some unknown force. When the scepter reached the clouds, it was as if it had hit a ceiling of glass: lightning shattered and splashed across the sky and thunder roared from above.

The foursome was all but lost when thunder shook the air. Lightning fell like bombs, tearing smoking holes in the ground. It sent the gerbits scattering like rats.

Brian, Ebil, Cassie and Tommy began staggering weakly to their feet with blood running from their open wounds. Then it rained with such force that it nearly knocked them down. In moments the water was so deep that the gerbits were swimming to safety.

Brian, exhausted, waded in the knee-deep water toward his brother.

"Brian?" Tommy mumbled, half dazed. Brian picked him up and carried him to the trunk of a mushroom, where its umbrella protected them from the pelting rain.

It was raining so hard he could scarcely see. Out of the wall of rain waded Cassie and Ebil.

"Are you all right?" Brian called to them.

"I've been better!" Ebil grumbled, but Cassie said nothing. They walked to them and Brian put his arm around Cassie to comfort her.

Their clothes were badly torn and blood flowed freely from open bites and hoof marks the gerbits had angrily delivered.

The rain slowed to a hard thundershower, but the water was now waist deep and was steadily rising. A mushroom Brian had cut for the fort floated by upside down.

Brian grabbed it and tested its buoyancy.

"Let's try getting in it," he suggested. "I think it'll hold all right."

He got in and helped the others crawl on. It was a little tipsy at first, but it held together well. The toadstool carried them along with the current, swirling them gracefully around mushroom stems as the rain cleansed their numb and bleeding wounds.

They rested as they drifted along, letting the mushroom go where it would.

Then they heard snorting.

"Look!" said Brian, pointing to a baby gerbit trying to swim to the mushroom. The gerbit struggled and grunted, all the time inhaling water.

Tommy shook his head. "He's gonna drown."

The little gerbit swam frantically next to the mushroom, but was unable to get his hooves up to climb in. Brian leaned over and lifted the little porker into the toadstool.

"What are you doing?!" Cassie exclaimed.

"Well . . . he would have drowned."

The gerbit snorted and choked, stumbling a little on the unsteady toadstool.

"As soon as he bites one of us, he goes!" Cassie said, a little uneasy about their fanged guest.

Ebil laid back and hummed softly in varying pitches, as the mushroom carried them through the night. The gerbit wobbled around, then finding a good spot it circled and laid down exhausted.

Cassie snuggled next to Brian and whispered, "Maybe he's not one of those nasty gerbits."

"Maybe they're not all so bad once you get to know them," he said softly.

The toadstool rode the flowing current, turning quietly under mushroom tops, ducking in and out of the night rain . . .

Chapter Nine

The Winds End

When daylight arrived the four were still drifting in their upside-down mushroom. It had proven itself a good boat and had carried them into a wide river while they slept. The banks were overgrown with trees and thick leafy plants. Swollen snakes dangled from overhanging branches as the mushroom drifted near shore. The water was warm and green with steam rising off its surface.

Cassie stretched her cramped leg and rubbed the soreness out of it. "Let's go ashore," she suggested.

"We'll go ashore just as soon as the snakes get a little smaller, Cassie," Brian said politely as he splashed river water on his wounds.

"You can protect us and besides, they probably don't bite," she said.

"They probably swallow you whole," Brian grumbled. Tommy and Ebil laughed as Cassie grinned and leaned back.

"Snort, Snort . . . Gnort!" said the gerbit as he curiously sniffed the uninviting water. The piglet snorted and rolled on his back, wiggling as Brian scratched his soft tummy.

"Look at the gerbit," Brian chuckled. "We've been adopted."

Ebil leaned over the side of the mushroom and twirled his knobby fingers in the soupy water. "There's an island up ahead," he said, motioning with his head.

Through the morning haze they could see the distinct outline of a small island that rose out of the middle of the river.

"I wonder if anybody lives there?" Tommy asked.

"Doesn't look like it," said Brian. "You know, it seems like I may have had a dream about a place like this once."

Ebil laughed getting Brian's attention, and then said, "Most realities are fantasies first."

Cassie smiled at Brian. "Was I in your dream?"

The wind off the river kicked up an unearthly mist that spun around them. A breath of air spoke. "Follow me . . . follow me, my friends, for the key." The wind swirled around them once more, then blasted straight in toward the small island.

"This is it! This is the place the wind has led us, Brian," said Cassie.

"I hope this wasn't a mistake; I hope we can get back home somehow," he said. The mushroom spun in the current and Brian caught a glimpse of something moving in the sky.

"Look, look! Back here," he pointed. "Nimbus!"

Red clouds hovered low over the river, oozing through the air as they sped toward them.

"Swim for it!" Cassie shrieked.

"Wait!" Brian stammered. "Wait! They're slowing, the clouds aren't coming any closer."

"They're not coming after us? I don't get it."

"Nimbus is only afraid for good reason," said Ebil.

They kept a close eye on the hovering clouds, as the current pushed them up to the sandy bank of the small island. The gerbit snorted and leaped into the shallow water as the rest of them stumbled out of the mushroom and splashed to shore.

A tower jutted out of the distant mist. "Do you see the tower?" said Brian? "Someone lives here!"

"This place is creepy," said Tommy.

In shore about 40 feet stood bare black trees. Blackbirds squatted on jagged dry branches. Beneath the trees grew a dense thicket. The birds fluttered and squawked as the foursome looked around.

Part of the thicket had been cut away and a path led through the trees and brush toward the tower.

"Everyone stay close," Brian cautioned as they started up the path.

Thousands of blackbirds filled the sky, circling and cawing, as thousands more stared at them from dark branches along the dirt path.

"All of these trees look like they're dead, and what's with all of these stupid birds?" said Cassie.

"I wish they'd shut up," Tommy sneered.

Ebil pranced along waving and smiling at the birds. He stopped to talk to one sitting on a branch. "Where are you now . . . where have you been?"

The bird cocked his head and cawed.

"You know," Ebil explained, "the further you travel in an eternity of empty space the more you will tend to remain in the same place."

"What ya doing, Ebe?" Brian asked.

"Tell me," said Ebil.

"Don't get strange on us now. We might need you."

"Can't . . . can't get . . . strange."

Brian frowned and continued up the long winding path. The closer they came to the tower the higher the path was built up off the ground. As they approached the tower Brian could make out a shiny glass bubble protruding out of the top of it at an angle.

Then, suddenly, a flash of bright white light erupted from the glass dome.

"I can't see," Cassie said, covering her eyes. It was so bright they all had to look away.

"Don't look at it," Ebil screeched.

The bright light began to slowly seep back into the dome and with it so did the light of day. The dome had absorbed all the light.

It turned dark and the sky was filled with stars and glowing moons.

"What's going on?" Brian asked. "This is amazing!"

"It's absorbing all the energy," said Ebil.

A breath of air brushed against Brian's face.

"The key lies within. Come in so we may begin."

"I hope we're not going to walk into something we'll regret. I don't like it," Said Brian.

"Those with power sacrifice pawns," said Ebil.

"No, not always," said Brian as they walked closer to the tower.

Blackbirds made almost invisible by the darkness cawed and rustled branches as they went by. The foursome walked to the end of the path and stood quietly in front of a huge iron door. Torches crackled on both sides of the entrance, casting distorted shadows on the tower wall.

The gerbit grunted impatiently, then nudged the heavy door open with his damp rubbery nose and trotted inside unafraid. It looked dark and strange inside so Brian took a torch off the wall as they entered.

Once inside the tower, Brian moved the torch around to get a better view of their surroundings.

Oval archways appeared to lead back into room after room. Big brass statues stood, hardened in the corners holding dripping candles. Gray mist floated in paper-thin layers. To the right was a circular stairway lit by candles along the wall.

"Follow the stairs," Ebil said gruffly.

"Yes," Cassie nodded. "Whatever it is we're looking for is probably up there."

"Everyone keep together," Brian urged.

The gerbit snorted.

"Yeah, you too," Cassie whispered, glancing down at the bumpy little beast.

They cautiously climbed the stairs.

"It doesn't look like anybody's home," Tommy said.

"I'm all around you," crackled an aged voice.

"Where?" Tommy asked.

"Why, everywhere!"

"I don't like it," Brian whispered faintly.

At the top of the stairs was a hexagon-shaped room containing thousands of old books. Candles held by brass stands and grizzly looking statues were scattered everywhere.

"Hello?" said Brian, looking around. He walked to a white marble circle engraved into the floor. The circle had another circle in the center; it resembled the green iris of a human eye. "Look at this," he said. "What do you think it means?"

Cassie came over. "I've seen it before, it means one with infinity or something. Whoever lives here might use this to magnify their powers."

"Indeed," said Ebil. "It is the symbol of Eur. It means no boundaries."

Directly above the marble circle was the glass dome protruding sideways out of the ceiling. It carried the same strange iris on it. Light from the dome shone down on the symbol on the floor.

Brian walked under the dome and looked up into the dark sky while Tommy ran his fingers down a row of books.

"Books, books and more books," he mumbled curiously.

The gerbit began snorting loudly at a shadowy corner on the other side of the room.

"What is it?" said Brian.

A thin wrinkled old man startled them when he moved out of the dark corner. His eye sockets were like black caverns, and he wore a long tattered robe. He had wild gray hair and a scraggly beard.

"Who are you? What do you want?" asked Cassie.

"Hi, Ebe," rasped the old man.

"Eurus" grinned Ebil as if he were meeting an old friend. So this is where you project from?"

"You know him?" Cassie asked, tugging on Ebil's arm for an answer.

"Yesss," Ebil hissed. "He is Eurus, an ole wind spirit, a wise dimension churning knower of the unknown, right hand to the great untouchable and unseen."

"Thanks, Ebe. That was nice," said the man, smiling faintly. I don't know about right hand, but I do a lot with the few tools I am given."

Brian noticed the man had a ring that carried the iris design. The old man toyed with the ring for a moment, then raised one of his long spider-like fingers and said, "There is much you need to know and something you must do if you wish to return home."

Brian cleared his throat. "Are you the one whose voice I heard in the wind?"

"Yes, it was I, and it was I who called you out on that dark night and led you to the pond," answered Eurus.

"Why?" Brian asked."

"You see, that pond of yours is a doorway between dimensions, between worlds. When Tommy entered this world it left a tangled void in your lives back home. I knew Tommy couldn't return by himself, so I summoned you and found you to be very suitable. I hoped with my help I could return both of you some day."

"Why would you care whether we return or not?" asked Brian.

"I'll try to explain it in a way you will best understand. Let's say you took a long rope that was perfectly straight. Okay, then throw the rope in a pile and wait a little while. When you go back and pick the rope up later, it will be all tangled up. The force that tangled the rope is a negative force. I am a positive force . . . I untangle things that get tangled. The membrane is a one-way door. No one has ever returned to your world. I saw the opportunity to untangle a tangle and took a chance."

Chapter Nine

"Hurfump," said Cassie. "Couldn't you just have zapped him back?"

"Oh my dear, my powers are not all that far reaching. I can affect my power on you now that you are here, but I can't control all space. I can only guide with my words, watch over and protect. Many times I must call on others to help."

"Then was it you who turned day into night?" Tommy asked.

"Yes, I needed to collect energy."

"And didn't you also save us from infinity?"

"I called on another who had more control in that space."

"Was it Grandma?" Tommy asked, afraid of the answer.

"Tommy, how could that be!" Brian blurted.

Cassie stood there thinking. "How about when I threw Leether's staff up in the clouds and it rained. Was that you?"

"No, it wasn't. The wand has an effect over Nimbus and when they came together it freed the rain and lightning and, with it, Leether from floating endlessly in infinity. He is a worthy adversary and now he tracks your every move and plots his next. You will have a small window of opportunity to beat him."

"How?" Cassie asked.

"It is beyond your comprehension."

Ebil stood in the back giggling.

"How come you have all these candles?" Tommy asked. Ebil burst out laughing.

"I like candles," the old man smiled.

"When are you gonna get us home?" said Brian.

The candles flickered off the old man's long thin face as he spoke. "The crystal will open the membrane, it is the key . . . it will turn an entrance into an exit.

"What's the big mystery?" Cassie asked. "Where is it?"

"I don't have it," Eurus said quietly.

Cassie sighed.

"You see," Eurus, continued, "the crystal is protected in a palace that lies on a plane between here and there."

"Somewhere out there," cackled Ebil, pointing at the dome.

"Brian, I will lead you on a journey to it. Your aura may go but your body may not."

"Huh?" said Brian wrinkling his forehead. "What's an aura?"

"All you are . . . all you really are is invisible. Your feelings, your thoughts, your memories, your inner self. This part of you can never be destroyed; a person's body may die but an aura will live on forever. You see, energy can never be destroyed; it only changes form. Your aura may go where your body cannot. Thus your body must remain."

"Don't go, Brian!" pleaded Cassie. "It sounds too weird!"

"Everything I've been through has been too weird," he replied.

Tommy shook his head. "I don't know if you should trust this guy. He looks like a bum. Just look at his robe. It looks like he slept in it."

"He'll talk you through it," said Ebil. Brian took a deep breath.

"What do I hafta do?"

"Stand in the center of the symbol of Eur and look up at the dome." Brian did as he asked, gazing up into the dark starlit sky.

The old man held his hands out, palms up, and spoke out to the stars.

"Sapphires of heavens . . . come to me, show your radiance . . . join with meee . . ."

In an instant it appeared as if he held all the stars in the sky in his withered hands. The tiny stars swirled, flashing and snapping from his fingertips. "Carry his aura on the wings of light and time," he echoed. Eurus thrust his hands upward and the stars exploded from his magical fingertips. Then a silver light illuminated Brian. He glowed for a moment as it hummed around him, glistening. Then the silver light left Brian's body, keeping its human shape and flew like a silvery ghost up through the glass dome. Cassie gasped, as Brian's body remained motionless on the symbol.

"Brian!" Cassie cried out, but Brian didn't move; he remained still and silent as if carved out of stone. "What have you done to him?" she whimpered.

"All that he is flew out through the dome; the body is all that remains," Eurus said quietly.

Meanwhile Brian's glowing silver aura sped through the sky. Led by the old man's words, he flew through swirling galaxies and exploding stars.

"I will lead you to the palace," he heard Eurus say as he sailed effortlessly through time and space to another place.

In a matter of moments he felt as if he were slowing down. He could see a strange palace floating alone in the starlit darkness. He couldn't tell the top from the bottom. It was different from anything he'd ever seen, though he could tell it was a palace.

"You may enter the palace halls."

Brian, feeling every bit like a silver ghost, coasted through the thick walls. He entered a long red hallway. Rectangular niches were cut out of the wall every 12 feet or so and men ten feet tall wearing black masks stood motionless in them.

Brian slipped quietly down the hall as he examined the masked giants in wonder. He wasn't sure if they were human but they stood erect, somehow frozen in time. Each of them held a luminous green club. The club was round and narrow at the top and round and wide at the bottom, much like a long trumpet.

"They are the guardians of the crystal," explained Eurus. "You will not wake them in your ghostly state. Follow the hallway ahead and take the crystal from its resting place. The crystal alone has the power to align dimensions."

Brian moved down the hallway, not stirring the air, and passed through a triangular opening into a big blue room. In the center of the room was a crystal as big as his fist mounted on a round stand. A strange machine hung over the top of the glassy gem. Sparks of white electricity snapped from the crystal into the machine. It looked like great amounts of energy were being drawn from it.

Brian gazed at the crystal for a moment, watching it rotate slowly, twinkling and sparking. Then he snatched the gem from its throne. The stand was unforgiving. Bolts of electricity shot out of it, bouncing off the walls.

"Oh, oh." Brian thought as he dashed out of the room and into the hall. Lights began flashing and odd alarms whined through the long corridors.

The guardians had been awakened and were now stepping out into the long hallway with their glowing green clubs.

"How can I get past them?" Brian wondered. "Can they hurt a ghost?"

The old man's voice whispered faintly, "You can touch, but you can't be touched."

"I hope you're right," Brian said, but his voice made no sound. He dashed down the long hallway at the creatures dressed in black. He flinched as they tried to pelt him with their glowing clubs. The weapons whisked through him, leaving him unharmed.

"I'm a real ghost!" Brian laughed to himself as he ran through the long line of frustrated, swinging guardians.

He leaped through the palace wall and was soon sailing through the open cosmos. Brian sped back through space to where he had left his friends. They could see him coming, a silver streak in the sky. He zapped in through the domed window and his aura entered the body it had left. The aura hummed for a moment, then faded back into him.

Brian stood there once again holding the flashing crystal.

When Cassie saw that Brian was himself again she ran to him and gave him a warm hug.

"You all right?" Tommy asked.

"Fine," Brian smiled as Cassie held him.

"What was it like?" Cassie murmured as she rested her soft cheek on his chest.

"Like being a ghost in someone else's dream," he replied.

Ebil was moving his head back and forth to some unknown song in his head. "Now you have the power to turn an entrance into an exit."

Brian, still standing on the symbol, held the crystal up and turned it slowly. The sparkling candlelight flashed off its clear surface.

"How does it work?" he asked.

Eurus explained, "When you get to the membrane, rotate it as you are now. When the crystal casts lights on the membrane similar to that of the symbol on the dome, the membrane will be reversed and you can get back through it. Even now, Leether anticipates our next move. We must hurry! Because you are now in my space I have control over you. With you here by me I have the power to drop you somewhere in the valley of tears. Hang on because I haven't done this for a while. You see, when energy is expended it always creates heat. It might feel a little warm".

Eurus held open his palms once again and stars lit from his fingertips. "The Mother of the Universe will carry you back on the wings of light, crisp and clean," he chanted. Brian felt himself succumbing to the old man's powers. For a moment everything was a hot, windy blur, then a flash of hot white light. The heat was unbearable, like standing in a furnace. The blur cleared and they all stood together in the grassy valley.

"Ouch!" said Ebil dropping the red-hot sword.

"Wow! I felt like I was getting barbecued!" said Tommy. "That was a little heat! I wonder what a lot of heat would have been like!"

"The crystal will lead you back to the membrane," said the old man's wispy voice.

It was smoking hot but look where we are! This is great!" said Brian.

Cassie looked up. "Eurus, I'm sorry for not trusting you."

The valley was cast in the shadow of the night and they could see the Tred's castle lit up by torches.

Brian felt the crystal tug forward, and he turned to lead them through the tall grass.

"We're going home, Tom!" he said softly, watching the wind gently lift Cassie's black hair as she fell in stride next to him.

Cassie saw a row of torches coming through the valley. "They must have spotted us!" she announced. "We probably lit up the whole valley when we landed!"

"I'll stay and hold them off," Ebil said. "'Leether has been waiting for us. They're coming fast."

"Are you crazy? You're coming with us," Brian barked, pulling on his arm.

They all began running, leaping clumsily through the tall grass.

"They're gaining," Brian yelled. The gerbit nudged Cassie as she staggered to stay on her feet. "Can you make it?" Brian asked.

"I'm okay! I just tripped, that's all. Come on," she said, running ahead of him.

They reached the edge of the forest.

"Which way to the membrane, Brian?" Tommy asked.

"Straight ahead through the trees."

Cassie turned and saw the row of torches getting closer.

"Come on Cassie!" Brian urged.

"Wait . . . listen!" she said.

A booming voice shattered the darkness: "Justice must be done!"

"It's Leether!" Brian whispered.

"It looks like my father is with him!" she said.

"It can't be far now; they won't get us," Brian assured her.

"Only if we hurry!" said Tommy. Brian felt the crystal jerk forward and he ran through the over-grown brush, dancing between the trees. The rest of them scrambled to keep up, dodging low branches.

At last, they came to the membrane. Brian fumbled with the glassy rock and held it up as he had been told. He focused the light on the jelly-looking entrance and turned it slowly.

The noise of the soldiers grew nearer.

"They aren't far off!" Tommy said as he watched Brian slowly rotate the crystal.

Then he got that perfect combination as the crystal cast the symbol of the Eur on the membrane. The membrane jiggled and jostled as it began to change.

"Come on!" said Brian, smiling at Cassie.

"No. I . . . I can't!" she said, "I'm afraid."

"Please come with us! I thought you'd come."

"No, I can't, I just can't," she said, beginning to cry. "I belong here."

Cassie gave Brian a warm embrace. "I'll miss you," she said. "You're the only one who ever really cared about me"

Brian gave her a kiss and looked into her eyes and held her soft face. "I need you," he said softly. "I don't know how but we will see each other again."

The gerbit grunted and nudged his leg.

"Come on, will ya!" Tommy pleaded.

Ebil took Cassie by the arm. "Time is tight," he said, "I'll protect her. Don't worry." Ebil gave Brian a toothy grin. "Remember, thoughtfulness is the shadow of wisdom." Then he hurried into the brush with Cassie and the gerbit running behind him.

"Take care of yourself, Brian," yelled Cassie.

"They're coming! They'll be here any second! Let's go!" Tommy begged, pulling Brian half into the membrane.

The knights were so close that their voices could be heard easily.

Brian yelled toward the area where Cassie had disappeared into the brush. "I'll come back for you someday!"

"I love you Brian," came her distant reply.

Tommy pulled Brian through the membrane to safety as Brian yelled, "I love you, too!"

Chapter Ten

Surprise Visit

Brian and Tommy fell away from the membrane, stumbling back into the dark tunnel.

"That was too close, Brian!" Tommy panted, his voice bouncing off the tunnel walls. "We almost blew it!"

"Tom, Brian asked, "think I'll ever see her again?"

"Well, you can always come back. You've still got the crystal, don't ya?"

"Yeah," Brian answered quietly. They turned and walked back through spongy moss. "Let's go home, Tom."

"I bet everyone thinks we're dead. I bet they think we drowned."

"I don't think this is gonna be easy to explain," said Brian as he worked to get the large crystal in his pocket.

139

They climbed over roots and stomped through the damp moss until they reached the tunnel's end. Brian and Tommy looked up at the circular opening in the bottom of the pond. Brian felt the water suspended across it. "Feels pretty warm, Tom. You go first and I'll follow."

"Forget it, Brian. You'll probably go back and look for Cassie after I go up."

"No, I won't, I promise . . . although that's not a bad idea," he said. He made a sling out of his hands to give Tommy a boost. Tommy placed his foot in Brian's steady hands, and took a deep breath.

"Ready?" Brian asked. Tommy nodded his cheeks puffed out like a hamster.

Brian arched his back and thrust his brother up into the warm depths of the pond. Brian stood motionless watching Tommy kicking frantically toward the surface and finally disappearing into the hazy water.

"I'll come back for you, Cassie," Brian said aloud, hoping somehow she could hear him or know his thoughts.

He gave a huge sigh. "Home again, home again . . . jiggity jig" he muttered as he reached up and grabbed the rim of the hole. Taking a deep breath, Brian lifted himself up into the warm water and somersaulted to get his entire body into it. He pushed hard off the bottom propelling his body upward. The surface seemed so far away. Brian's lungs burned and his body cried out to take a breath. He swam frantically for the shimmering sunlight far overhead. He finally broke through the shiny surface of the water and gasped for air.

Tommy was sitting on the raft, water dripping off his face. "What took ya so long? I was beginning to wonder."

"Hey, it's daytime!" Brian smiled. He could feel the familiar warmth of the sun on his face.

"It must be early morning," said Tommy looking at the position of the sun.

Brian turned over and floated on his back. "Boy, this really feels good; no one is chasing us anymore. What a relief. It feels so safe to be back home."

"Home is where we belong," said Tommy. Brian swam toward shore and Tommy dove off the raft behind him. They swam into shallow water and ran onto shore together.

A warm summer breeze whistled through the trees as a wispy voice said, "Throw the crystal in the center of the pond, and the doorway between worlds will be forever closed."

"No," said Brian, "then I'll never see Cassie again. Sorry, Eurus, I'm sure you understand, I just can't do that." Brian turned his back on the pond and started to walk away, then paused. "I'll be back and talk later," he said.

The two brothers walked home through the rolling grassy field. Tommy pushed the grass to one side as they walked along. "I bet Mom will be surprised," he said.

"That's an understatement!" Brian grinned.

They approached the familiar old farmhouse and crossed the back yard. Tommy opened the screen door like he'd done a thousand times before. It squeaked like it always did, and then slammed behind them.

"Mom?" Brian called as they stood apprehensively in the kitchen.

"Huh?" was the answer from another room. "Who . . . who's there?"

"Where are you, Mom?" Brian asked. They could hear something crash and break, then the sound of their mother running down the hall.

She burst into the kitchen where they stood dripping wet. "Haaa!" she screamed, holding her face. "Oh my God! Oh my God!"

"Mom!" called Tommy.

She screeched again and ran over to hug them. She cried, looked at them and nervously felt their faces as if to be sure they were real. "Are you all right?" she said, tears streaming down her face. "Where have you been?"

Tommy glanced at Brian.

Brian frowned. "It's hard to explain. We . . . we were lost."

"How? Where did you go?"

"It's a long story. Can we get into some dry clothes first?"

"Where did you get these funny bathrobes?" She felt the material. "Why are you all wet?"

"We'll try to explain it all to you," said Brian.

"I love you boys so much. You mean everything to me." She hugged them again and began to cry some more. "I refused to believe you two were dead!"

"We missed you Mom!" said Tommy.

"We love you too, Ma," said Brian. "I'm sorry we put you through so much pain."

"Where's Grandma?" Tommy asked.

"There's something I need to tell you," said Mrs. Hummel.

"Grandma!" said Brian, releasing his mother and rushing into the living room. He saw the old rocking chair slowly moving back and forth, facing the window.

Brian smiled with relief. "Grandma!" he called out. He approached the chair. His brief smile turned to a look of dismay as the empty chair moved back and forth in the breeze from the open window.

Tommy and Mrs. Hummel entered the living room still clutching one another.

Chapter Ten

"Boys, shortly after you left, your grandmother passed away."

"Oh no!" cried Brian.

"It was her!" Tommy burst out. "She saved us from death, she saved us from infinity, it was her . . . I knew it." He began to cry. "She loved us so much she saved us after she was dead."

"What?" their Mother asked completely bewildered.

"Uh . . . we'll change our clothes now, Ma," said Brian. "What's for lunch?"

"Uh, I don't know. I'll go look." Completely stunned, she turned and walked weakly to the kitchen.

They went to their rooms and put on dry clothes. Brian carefully hid the glassy crystal in his wooden trunk between some old blankets.

When they came out, their mother was already on the phone spreading the news. "No, they're alive," she insisted. "I swear it! I'm okay . . . No . . . they walked right through that door, both of them. They didn't say; I have no idea where they've been."

"Brian," said Tommy, "Mom forgot to fix lunch."

"She's been on the phone. Just make a sandwich," he suggested.

They sat down at the table with peanut butter and jelly and began making sandwiches.

Mrs. Hummel hung up and sat down with them. "Now," she said, leaning forward, "what in the world happened to you?"

Brian and Tommy looked at one another. "Mom," said Brian, "we were in another place, another world that we got to by going through a hole in the bottom of the pond."

"What!" she screeched. "Do you think this is funny?"

"I'm not laughing," said Brian.

"Can't you see how hard this has been for me?"

"We're sorry, Ma," said Tommy.

"Didn't you realize that while you were off gallivanting God knows where, people might think you're dead? First Tommy is supposed to have drowned, then Brian disappears and we find the old lantern floating in the pond. Of course the police can't find any trace of you, 'no bodies found' they said. Oh, the horrible stories people made up. Do you boys realize there are tombstones in the cemetery with your names on them? What really happened? Why won't you answer me?" she screamed, bursting into tears.

"Just calm down, Ma," said Brian. "Everything's gonna be all right now. We'll talk all about it. You know we'd never intentionally hurt you. The main thing is that we're all together now. We're all together."

Tommy and Brian stayed around the house all day, thought about all they had been through then went to bed early.

By their second day home, everyone in the community had heard of their bazaar reappearance.

Brian sat on his bed lacing up his tennis shoes.

"Brian," said a soft voice. He looked up at his mother in the doorway. "I think it's time you told me where you two were," she said. "What happened to you?"

"I'll tell ya Ma, but you're gonna think I'm nuts."

"Go on."

"Well, there is some kind of doorway between dimensions that we went through on the bottom of the pond." Mrs. Hummel nodded frowning slightly. "We got through and couldn't get back. There's a whole other world there, a strange world and this girl named Cassie that I'll really miss."

"You're serious aren't you?" she said, puzzled.

"Yes . . . yes I am. You know I have never lied to you."

"Brian, you're my son and I love you, but I just don't know what to think anymore."

"I know Ma, I don't expect you to understand. I wouldn't believe it either. Now I need to get out of this house. I'm gonna give Dave a call."

"I just talked to his mother on the phone. She said a bunch of the boys went to play baseball at the school."

"Great!" he said, then yelled down the hall. "Tom, I'm going to play baseball." Tommy peered around the corner from the kitchen.

"Can I come?" he asked meekly.

"Of course," Brian said, waving him on.

They ran through the grassy field and took a short cut through the woods, then walked up to the diamond where the boys were playing. It was a scrubby field with scratched-in bases. The weeds had been mowed to make it easier in the outfield. The game was in progress when Brian and Tommy arrived. They felt a little tense, wondering what kind of reception they would receive.

The boys stopped playing and turned their attention to them.

"Look, it's dead man!" said Dan, stepping up to bat.

"The living dead," Toby laughed, walking stiff like Frankenstein.

"A couple of Zombies like on that one movie," said Joey.

Brian and Tommy waited for them to stop teasing.

"No, they're the creatures from the deep!" said Dan and they all laughed again.

"Aw, cut it out!" Brian interrupted. Joey Hasselback came up to Tommy and examined his face.

"Aren't you supposed to be dead?" he asked.

"Sorry to disappoint ya," Tommy grumbled.

"They do look a little pale, feel to see if he's cold," said Dave. They all laughed mockingly at them.

"Knock it off!" yelled Brian.

"Well then, where were ya?" Toby asked.

"Uh, we were kidnapped," Tommy blurted.

"By who? Pirates or Gypsies?" They all laughed again.

"Look!" Brian stammered. "You don't know what we've been through, so why don't ya just shut up!"

"Look Brian!" said Dave, becoming visibly angry.

"You don't know what we've been through. First, we hear you guys are dead. Drowned in that evil pond. Can't find the bodies, pond musta swallowed ya whole! Everybody gets all creeped out. A week and a half goes by, then we hear that you mysteriously reappear. You don't look dead to me! So where have you been? If you guys thought this was some kind of a funny joke, you're wrong. Were ya playing a Huck Finn? I don't know about anybody else, but I'll admit I felt really bad when I thought you were dead. And now we find out that you two bums were laughing behind our backs the whole time. Until you can explain why you did it, get lost. We can't use ya!"

Brian sighed. "You know us better than that; come on, Tom," he said placing his hand on Tommy's shoulder. They turned and headed back home.

"We should tell 'im, Brian," said Tommy, while kicking a daisy from its stem.

Brian shook his head. "They wouldn't believe it. Would you? They'll really think we're a couple of jerks if we do; it's bad enough already. I'd really like to tell somebody though. Maybe I'll write a book."

Chapter Ten

Tommy was silent for a moment his head down, watching his worn tennis shoes plod along, one in front of the other. "We gotta tell 'em somethin'!" he said.

"Kidnapped by gypsies' ain't gonna make it, Tom. Everything'll fall in place," said Brian. "It always does. We'll just wait it out. It'll get back to normal and they're still our friends . . . I think."

The brothers spent the rest of the day hanging around the house. After a day of sitting around, Brian went into his room and dug the crystal out of the trunk. He sat on his bed and examined it closely. He held it in front of the window and let the light from the setting sun pass into it. It sent glorious prisms of light around the room.

"What ya doing?" Tommy asked, leaning against the doorway. Brian looked up, startled.

"Oh . . . uh, I'm just thinking about Cassie. I wonder what she's doin'." He glanced at Tommy. "Close the door; I don't want Mom to see this rock."

Tommy closed the door. "What are you gonna do with it?"

"Don't know," Brian said, tossing it casually in the air. The rock slapped into his palm, then he jerked his hand back as if he'd been poked with a pin. "Ow!" He looked very puzzled.

"Can I see it?" Tommy asked.

"Just a minute. I think I got a shock when I caught it," Brian answered. He looked at it closely, then shook it like a salt shaker over his nightstand. A small bolt of lightning snapped free of the crystal, burning a small smoking hole in the table.

"Damn! How am I gonna explain this?"

"Brian, Mom's gonna kill you," Tommy warned. "You'd better get rid of that thing. We could get hurt."

"No, it's okay. Want to see it now?" he said, handing the crystal to his brother.

"No! I don't want a shock!"

"Don't worry," said Brian. "It won't hurt you unless you shake it at something . . . I think." Tommy scowled and Brian saw his disapproval. "I'll put it away for now, Tom."

Brian put the crystal back in the trunk between the blankets. He then locked it and hid the key in his baseball mitt.

Brian plopped face down on the bed and stared at the headboard as if there were some answers there.

"What's the matter, Brian?" Tommy asked.

"Aw, geeze. Cassie's gone. Mom thinks we're weird and all of our friends think we're a couple of jerks. I know it'll get better, but it's all kind of a strain."

Tommy grinned. "If Ebil were here, I bet he'd tell us some rhyme or say something that would help."

"Yeah. For someone who was insane, he was pretty sane sometimes."

"That sounded like something he'd say," laughed Tommy. Brian chuckled too.

"Close the curtain would ya, Tom? It's getting dark."

Tommy moved to the window and began to pull the curtain cord. To his surprise, he saw an ugly pushed-in face wearing a spiked helmet looking in the window at him.

"Haa! He screeched, jumping away from the window. "It's a Black Knight!" he stammered.

Brian turned over just in time to see busted boards and glass fragments exploding from the window.

The knight chopped his way in, leaving a hole where the window used to be. The large sword whistled around the room destroying everything as Tommy dove for safety. Brian looked on in disbelief. The knight took a swing at Brian as he scrambled off the bed. The sword came down and buried itself deeply in the headboard. While the knight tugged to get the sword free, Brian yanked off his bedspread and threw it over the knight's head. He pulled the cloth down hard, catching it on the armored spikes.

"Get my bat!" Brian screamed. "Tom, get the bat!"

Tommy quickly emerged from the closet with the bat. While the knight struggled to get free, Tommy took a few home-run swings at the knight. The knight stumbled, freeing his sword, but still caught up in the blanket.

Brian took the bat from his brother and finished the job. He pounded the knight down, smashing him unconscious on the bedroom floor.

"Tommy! What's happening?"

"They must have come up through the pond."

"I've got to throw the crystal in the pond. I never thought that they could or even might come up. Damn! Why didn't I think of it? This is terrible!"

"Ahaaa! Help . . . oh my God! Help me," a familiar voice screamed outside. They looked out the demolished window and saw Leether and a Black Knight dragging their horror-stricken mother toward the pond.

"Oh-no! NO!" Tommy hollered in panic. He picked up the knight's sword and sprang through the window.

"All hell has broken loose," Brian thought to himself. "Tom! wait!" he called out, but Tommy never looked back as he ran after his mother.

Brian grabbed the bat but suddenly realized it would be no match for Leether's powers and neither would the sword.

"The crystal!" He said aloud, grabbing for his baseball mitt. He fumbled for the hidden key. "I've got to hurry," he thought. "A second could make all the difference." He charged the trunk with the key and jammed it roughly into the tarnished old lock. He rotated the key round and round until the key snapped with a click and the lock band popped open.

He dug frantically through the blankets for the magical rock. "I can't find it!" he cried. Then he saw just a small twinkle. Brian plunged his hand down between the blankets. "Got it!" he said, yanking out the huge diamond.

"Brian!"

"Huh?" He turned and saw Cassie through the shattered window frame.

"Brian! They've got your mother!"

"Cassie, what are you doing here?'

"I saw them going through the membrane so, I had to warn you but now I'm too late! You'd better hurry!"

He jumped to his feet and leaped like a hurdler through the devastated window.

"Run! Run!" yelled Cassie. "Catch them! Don't worry about me. I'll catch up. Hurry!"

He ran with all he had, his heart pounding like an iron hammer in his chest. Tall grass slapped against him as he chased them. He could hear his mother screaming far off in the distance. Brian, stunned by the nightmare unfolding before him, raced after his mother and brother.

He could hear swords clashing ahead as he neared, and then he saw Tommy block a heavy blow and fall to the ground.

The knight glanced up and saw Brian coming. He raised his sword like an executioner to finish Tommy before taking on Brian. Tommy held his sword up defensively, anticipating the blow.

Brian snapped the crystal hard at the knight, concentrating on his glistening armor chest plate. A crisp white bolt of energy crackled from the crystal and blasted the knight hard in the chest. The knight fell, smoking, to the grassy turf.

"Come on, Tom!" Brian screamed as he ran by him. Tommy scurried to his feet while his mother's voice cried in the distance.

Brian jumped through the heavy brush surrounding the pond. He could see Leether and his mother waist-deep in the water.

Leether held Mrs. Hummel's short brown hair with one hand as she thrashed violently to get free.

"Brian! Help!" she cried. Her white-knuckled hand clenched Leether's arm. She struggled to get away from the vice-like grip that pulled her into deeper water.

"Brian! Do something. Get help!" she yelled to him.

Leether looked at Brian and smiled broadly. "Ah, my lamb," he said calmly. "Surprised to see me once again? I knew you'd come."

"Brian," whispered Tommy from behind a bush. "What should I do?"

"Sneak around behind him."

"Justice must be done for Nimbus!" the priest began to chant. "Gelidity requiem," he murmured, raising his free hand in the air. The water began bubbling lively around him.

"Let her go, you psycho!" Brian screamed. Concentrating on Leether's midsection, he snapped the rock at him. A burst of bright white light lit out of the crystal like an angry rocket. Leether blocked the bolt with the palm of his free hand.

"Ha!" he said smiling, "clever weapon, but it is a mistake to resist my will. Rufecent phantom, ghostlike brume. Seep amongst this murky water. Rufous smaze, cast your haze. Justice must be done for you, justice must be done."

Red mist began popping out of the bursting bubbles. The crimson haze rose slowly, forming a thin cloud above the priest.

"Brian," whispered Cassie. Brian looked back and saw Cassie crawling up behind him, hidden in the tall grass.

"What's Leether doing?" Brian asked.

"I think he's bringing Nimbus up through the pond to attack us."

"Let her go!" Brian demanded. "What is it you want from us?"

"Why, your very lives!"

Brian took a few steps closer and shook another bolt loose from the crystal. It crackled through the air and a thunderclap sounded as Leether stopped it with his palm.

Leether laughed tauntingly. "Don't you see? Thunder and lightning are my weapons. You're beaten. You're all going to die, you're all coming with me."

"Keep on shocking him," Cassie suggested. "Maybe we can wear him down."

Brian reeled back and snapped the crystal at him once again, but this time Leether blocked it and sent the thrust of energy reeling back.

Brian dove for cover as the bristling charge of electricity singed his airborne leg, leaving a smoking hole in his pants. He clawed his way into the brush and Cassie patted out the smoldering cloth.

Leether laughed wildly, still holding a handful of Mrs. Hummel's hair.

"Get . . . . get help," she panted, pale and tired.

"Rise! Rise, rufecent phantom!" Leether chanted, his fingers stretched toward the darkening sky. The water bubbled angrily around him. The red mist rose, condensing into a thick, red ooze that hung over the pond.

Tommy slipped unnoticed into the water behind the priest. He paddled silently across the pond, pulling the long sword behind him. He eased himself through the water, moving nearer and nearer, to Leether's back. When his toes grazed the bottom, he knew he would be able to stand. He was so frightfully close to the obsessed priest that the water bubbled up in his face. The red mist burst all around him, he choked and felt it burning in his throat.

"Nimbus shall have what is his," he heard the priest bellow. The red mist continued to choke him and the haze stung his eyes. He knew he was close, so close he could hear his mother whimpering but he couldn't see her through the bubbling haze.

The mist was making him nauseous and dizzy. He stood up to get his face out of the bubbles and lifted the sword high out of the water.

Leether quickly turned and saw Tommy staggering just out of striking range. "Ah, little one!" Leether laughed, seeing the boy try to hold up the sword. "You will be the first to go!"

Crack! A charge of energy snapped solidly into the priest's back, catching him off guard. His body quaked absorbing the full impact of the charge.

"Yes!" Cassie screamed.

Leether fell limply into the pond. His smoking body sank slowly back into the churning water as the red ooze began to follow him down.

"He's gone!!" Tommy cried out, swimming over to embrace his mother. The red ooze continued following Leether down into the deep.

Brian and Cassie held one another as Tommy and his mother walked ashore and collapsed next to them.

"Are you all right, Ma?" Brian asked, kneeling next to her.

"Yeah . . . yes," she panted. "What's happening?"

"I think it's all over now," he answered.

They sat on the bank together watching the last of the red ooze and smoke sink back into the gurgling pond.

A battered Black Knight crashed through the brush carrying another knight on his back.

"Haaa!" Mrs. Hummel screamed, clutching her face. The knight ran full tilt into the pond and stumbled into deeper water. The knights' dark shapes sank and disappeared with a splash and a ripple.

"They're all gone now. They're all gone, forever, I think," Brian muttered.

The wind whistled through the trees and Brian knew Euris was about to speak.

"Throw the crystal. Throw it in the center of the pond. Close the door forever," then voice faded into the wind.

Brian turned to Cassie. "Cassie, you know if I throw the crystal in the pond you can never go back. You'll stay here forever.

She looked into his eyes and smiled. "Go ahead, throw it. I want to stay." She nuzzled against his cheek. "I want to be anywhere you are!"

Brian looked at the shiny rock one last time. "Here goes!" he announced. He leaned back and lobbed the crystal high in the air. It came down in the center of the pond with a splash!

Soon the pond began flashing with light and a pure white mist lifted off the surface of the water.

"Let's go home," said Brian, taking Cassie's hand.

"This is the girl you talked about?" said Mom. She gave Cassie a tight hug. "Are you okay, dear?"

"I am now," said Cassie.

"Where's she gonna sleep?" asked Tommy.

"My room," laughed Brian, and Cassie grinned.

"Brian, we'll talk about it when we get home. Perhaps Grandma's room."

And they all began the journey back home . . .

THE END FOR NOW . . .

A note from the author

This story spent many years in the form of typed pages in a notebook. The notebook got passed on from friend to friend. I told everyone who read it that if it ever got into print I would put their names in the back of the book. Keeping my promise, the following people read my story even before it was a book. Their encouragement inspired me to keep going.

Jordan Stricklen	Justin Stricklen	Cheryl Stricklen
Dan Sharp	Hayley Cornelisse	Robin Crossman
Kelly Felker	Garry Quakkelaar	Tracy Roper
Libby Herron	Stephanie Sabo	Beth Dykhouse
Scott Hummel	Steven Hummel	Kristine Kayser
Richard Kirchhoff	Joseph Kirchhoff	Aren Smith
Rose Cucinella	Susan Reister-Tomkins	Barb VanderMolen
Liz Sawle	Sherry Barnes	Linda Ruonavara
Debbie Monterussso	Kelly Peska	Eric Tomkins
Katie Essner	Grace Essner	Theresa Roland
Melissa Jaworowski	Juanita Hafer-Dreyer	Paul Beauchamp
Patricia Gaines	Trudy Aebig	Wendy Pressey
Colleen Drozd	Ellen Taylor	Bill Hekker
Nate Horling	Jill Horling	Randy Brinks
Susan Brown	Kim Bouma	Kim Davis

Kaye Bouma	Patrick Sikkema	Jenny Baucha
Gladys Devlaminck	Kim Brandt	Doug Brubaker
Sally Veldkamp	Shelly Medina	Mary Rodschafer
Sue Lock	Alan Mrozinski	Kristin Fidler
CC Chang	Cindi Baltimore	Liz Sullivan
Brenda Leonard	Missi Keiser	Jody Naimo
Holly Harper	Amy DeVries	Renee Veldman
Rick Royston	Sergio Royston	Brandon Royston
Christina Thelen	Elaine Hudson	Rebecca Dykhuis
Karen Walsh	Mike Moll	Catey Reed
Bree Byle	Ann Byle	Pat Bruwer
Sandy Gatens	Mary Bernthal	

Printed in the United States
148089LV00002B/90/A